STAGECOACH WEST

WILLIAM HEUMAN

SAGEBRUSH
Large Print Westerns

First published in the United States by
Fawcett Gold Medal

First Isis Edition
published 2020
by arrangement with
Golden West Literary Agency

A catalogue record for this book is available
from the British Library.

ISBN 978-1-78541-849-5

Published by
Ulverscroft Limited
Anstey, Leicestershire

Set by Words & Graphics Ltd.
Anstey, Leicestershire
Printed and bound in Great Britain by
T. J. International Ltd., Padstow, Cornwall

This book is printed on acid-free paper

CHAPTER
ONE

The Utes had stripped Grady Mulvane as cleanly as a cat would strip the meat off a fish. They'd left nothing except eighteen blue-tipped arrows embedded in the body of his partner, Joe Beauford, and only the last one had been fatal because this was the way of an Indian.

The August sun was hot, and the sweat trickled down Grady's lean face, blinding him so that he cursed savagely as he scooped out a shallow grave into which he could roll poor Joe's body. He cursed the heat, and he cursed the Utes, and he cursed this wild forsaken country between the foothills and the higher escarpments of the Rockies. He'd persuaded Joe to come out here because he'd known that this was good wild-horse country; he'd seen the fast-moving herds many times, and he'd been right because they'd been doing well until the band of Utes rode out of some hidden defile while Grady was a dozen miles to the north, trying to push a small band of mustangs toward the brush and pole V-shaped corral they'd built with such painstaking effort earlier in the spring.

Thinking back on it now, Grady realized that the Utes had been watching them all the time from the higher hills, letting them sweat, letting them drive the wild ones into the corral, letting them tear their insides to pieces as they broke the animals to the saddle, and then when they were ready and only one man was at the shack, they'd moved in.

Grady glanced toward the hills into which they'd disappeared, and into which he'd be going. He'd follow their trail even though there were seven of them in this band, and the odds were not good. He owed that much to Joe Beauford, a good partner.

They'd killed Joe out near the corral in which they'd held the half-broken ponies, almost fifty of them, and they would have brought a fair price back east a ways. Because the Utes had even taken their digging tools, Grady used a sharpened stick to dig the grave, and the work was slow, and the delay was agony because he wanted to get some of the Utes in the sight of his Winchester. But he owed this much to Joe, and he didn't expect to be coming back.

He paused once to squat on his heels in the hot sun and roll a cigarette. The shack in which they'd lived had collapsed as he rode up less than half an hour ago. It was a heap of burning ashes now. The circular corral was still here, but empty. Grady had his gray gelding; he had his Winchester, and he had a Colt .44. That was all; these comprised his total possessions, aside from a few coins in his pocket.

Only the previous night he'd been talking to Joe about this. Both of them were stone-broke except for the wild ones in the corral, but they'd expected to sell the wild ones when they'd driven them east, and with

MR

STAGECOACH WEST

Riding into town with pennies to his name after a
venture to round up wild horses ends with his pard
riddled with arrows and everything they owned in

the   the
figu   But
the   the
seas   a
pro   cal
Cor   for
clue   ave
bee   ld.
Wit   ty,
and   ing
rob   cut
out   zle
of a

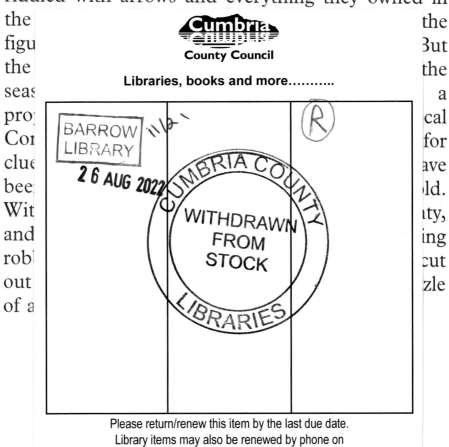

the proceeds they'd agreed to buy blooded stock and raise horses.

"We need plenty of horses out in this country," Joe had said. "Get some of them Morgans, Grady. Fellow up Flat Buttes way had a pair of 'em. There's horses."

Grady flipped away the half-smoked cigarette and went to work with the sharpened stick again. Once or twice he glanced at the inert body sprawled on the ground a few feet away, but looking at Joe this way made him uncomfortable. It was not really Joe Beauford on the ground; Joe had gone away. This was a stranger he had to bury, a stranger with eighteen arrows embedded in his bleeding body.

In another half an hour Grady had finished his work. He had to break off some of the arrow shafts because they protruded above the rim of the hole he'd dug for Joe. He didn't even have a blanket into which he could wrap the body of this stranger who had died two hundred miles west of the nearest town. He cut a few cottonwood branches from a nearby tree, strewed them on the body, pushed back the dirt with a flattened board he retrieved from the fire, and then was ready to go. He rolled stones on top of the soft dirt to prevent the coyotes or timber wolves from digging up the body.

He tried to think of some kind of prayer to say before he rode off, but he was not a praying man, and the best he could come up with was, "God bless you, Joe Beauford — " not the arrow-riddled piece of clay under the soft dirt in front of him, but the strong, browned Joe Beauford who loved horses as Grady Mulvane loved horses, and who would now have to ride them in another place.

It was an hour past noon when Grady lifted himself into the saddle and pushed west toward a defile in the hills. He figured that the Utes had at least two hours on him, which was not too much considering the fact that they would be pushing half a hundred skitterish, half-wild mustangs ahead of them through rough country. He anticipated catching up with some of them before nightfall, because the gray was a big horse with plenty of bottom, and because he intended to push the gelding until it dropped, if necessary.

He would not meet up with all the Utes who had been in on the murder of Joe Beauford. He'd spent enough time in these hills to know how the Utes and other mountain and plains tribes operated. They would split up, and then split again until a man wouldn't know which trail to take, and all the time the trails would be getting colder and colder, and more difficult to follow as the smaller bands moved through rough country. Grady had seen it happen with army details following recalcitrant bands; he had seen young officers driven to distraction by these constantly dividing trails.

The trail of the Ute band was easy to follow. Grady pushed the gray along at a fairly fast pace, remembering to ride with caution even this early in the chase. The Utes had another cute little trick of dropping one of their number behind to form an ambush, and a rider coming on could expect to take an arrow through the chest at very close range.

4

The seven Utes made their first split when they were five miles from Grady's camp. They were crossing a high mountain meadow, studded with flowers. At the far end of the meadow four went toward the northwest with a part of the horse band, and three went toward the southwest. Grady stayed with the three who went south, hoping that these three would stay together. It was almost a foregone conclusion that the other four would split in pairs later on, which would give him only two men to tackle when he was ready to jump them. He wanted more than two. He wanted all of them if he could get them, but barring this, as many as possible.

They were still climbing, the Utes finding the easy routes through the mountains, crossing mountain streams, heading due south for a while, and then turning west again. There were no ambuscades as yet, and he didn't think he would run into any. The three Utes ahead of him would stay close together from now on. They had no doubt by this time ascertained that only one man was following them, and this they had not been sure of in the beginning, when there was always the possibility Grady had been able to find help.

Still, he was carrying a Winchester rifle, and this gun the Utes feared because most of them would still be using bows and arrows, although a sprinkling of rifles was now trickling in to the mountain tribes.

The sun set early in the mountains, and it was nearly dusk when Grady followed the Utes into a deep canyon which ran north and south. They were headed north again now, having made a wide circle, and he was wondering if they intended rejoining the first group

5

before they rode into their camp. An Indian never liked to ride into camp alone after a victorious coup. This bunch had taken a white scalp and come in with a band of horses. It was reasonable to assume that they would meet up again to put on full warpaint, and then ride into the home camp chanting their song of victory — victory over poor Joe Beauford, who had never even known they were coming.

Pushing on hard now, and moving along the west wall of the canyon in the deep shadows, Grady was confident that he would catch up with the three Utes before darkness set in. Already, he could dimly see shapes up ahead, but since he was hugging the dark shadows along the west wall, he was positive they could not see him.

The canyon widened as they moved north until it was over a mile wide, and Grady noticed that the Utes had edged over toward the east rampart. He made his plans, then, without any hesitation. An Indian liked surprise even less than a white man. They could fight hard, and they could fight well when they made their own fight, but when a fight was suddenly thrust upon them and they were at a temporary disadvantage, they cracked more quickly than the white man.

Pushing the gray gelding hard now, Grady drew abreast of the three Utes and the band of mustangs ahead of them. He could see them vaguely across the canyon floor, but they could not see him as he still rode in the deep shadows. The hoofs of twenty-five odd ponies, along with their own mounts, drowned out the hoofbeats of Grady's gray.

When he was a quarter of a mile ahead of the band, he suddenly left the canyon wall and shot out across the front of the moving band. They were all riding in murky shadows now, and the Utes never saw him until the ponies they were driving split to go around him.

He was waiting for them, then, the Colt gun in his hand, because this was to be at close range, and he needed plenty of firepower. The three Utes were a dozen yards apart as they rode, and the middleman came upon Grady very suddenly, driving his pony straight toward him as Grady sat astride the gray gelding waiting for him.

Grady saw the feather in the Ute's hair outlined against the night sky. He heard the Indian's startled yell, and he saw a gun coming up, and then he shot the Ute through the chest at a range of less than five yards.

Grady swerved the gray and rode straight for the Ute on his left. Bending low in the saddle, he heard an arrow whip past his left ear, and then the big gray crashed into the smaller Indian pony, sending it staggering; and as the Ute fought to keep his seat, Grady fired twice, and he was sure both bullets were deadly.

The third Ute had shot on up ahead after the fleeing ponies, and Grady went after him grimly, thinking of Joe Beauford now, maybe running like this, but with Ute arrows stuck in him, running aimlessly, running in agony. Grady had seen his tracks, and the blood. He kept after the Ute up ahead, and he could feel the gray straining beneath him.

7

The big horse had run hard today, and it had run far, but it did not have much more to run. Considerably faster than the Ute pony, the gray drew up on the fleeing Indian in leaps and bounds.

This man carried bow and arrow, too, and once Grady saw him turn and whip an arrow back at his pursuer. At fifteen yards Grady could have shot him in the back, and he had no compunction about shooting him in the back after having seen what they'd done to Joe Beauford — but this one he wanted to close with.

It was foolish, and he knew it; he was liable to get a knife in the stomach and lose his scalp because a cornered Ute was as dangerous as a mountain lion, but he was still going to close with this man. Shooting a man from a distance, any distance, was one thing, but killing him at close range was another.

The two riders pounded on across the canyon floor, passing some of the fleeing ponies Grady had broken during the summer. He even recognized one of them in the dim light, a spotted brown and white animal with white forelegs, a truly vicious animal which would buck every time a man put a saddle on him, and probably would remain that way till the day it died.

For the first time that day, Grady put the spurs to the gray, something he seldom did. Surprised, the big gelding snorted and shot ahead, coming almost abreast of the fleeing Ute.

Gray had holstered the Colt gun. The Winchester was in the rifle boot on the other side of the saddle. He let his body fall to the right, and he reached out, his fingers entwining themselves in the coarse, greasy hair of the Indian. He was out of the saddle, then, clinging to the Ute, dragging him from his pony. Both men hit the ground hard, rolling as their horses pounded on, but Grady still clung to the long hair.

He managed to get to his feet first, and he let go of the hair and smashed hard at the Ute's face, hitting him squarely on the nose. He could hear and feel the bones crackle as the nose was broken, and the Ute screamed from the sudden pain as he fell backward.

He had a knife out, though, as Grady lunged after him, slipping a knife from his own belt. The Ute's hunting knife ripped open Grady's shirt, grazing the flesh as Grady struck him with his body, knocking him to the ground. The smell of the Indian was strong upon him as they rolled on the ground, each man struggling furiously to grasp the other's knife hand. The smell was the smell of the unwashed, the smell of buffalo hides, and chip and woodfires, and the smell of rancid bear grease in the hair.

The Ute was a fairly big man, although not quite as tall as Grady, who stood at an even six feet, and even with the shock of the smashed nose he was still strong. Grady felt the wet, hot blood from the streaming nose as they struggled on the ground, and then he had the Indian's knife hand pressed hard to the ground, and his own knife was free as he came up on top of his man.

He struck down three times with the blade, driving the knife in at a point a little below the neck. After the third blow, the Ute's body went slack. The hand Grady had been pinning to the ground became limp, and the knife fell from it.

9

His body trembling from the exertion, Grady picked up the Ute's knife and tossed it away into the darkness. He rolled off the man, rolled again until he was three or four paces away, and then he lay still on his back, taking long, deep, agonized breaths.

Overhead, he could see stars coming out in the dark vault of the sky. A crescent moon was swinging up over the east rampart of the canyon. Off in the distance he could hear his running ponies, scattering now as they reached the broken ground at the far end of the canyon. The gelding had undoubtedly stopped because he'd tossed the reins over the animal's head before making his dive at the Ute.

The Indian on the ground died slowly. Grady could hear the heavy breathing which became more and more faint. He listened carefully as he lay on the ground, and he strained his ears, but how the breathing had stopped, and the man was dead.

Maybe wherever Joe Beauford was, this fact satisfied him; maybe it made no difference; maybe he was not even aware of it, but Grady Mulvane knew one thing. It had had to be done.

For fully ten minutes he lay on the ground until the strain had gone out of his body. He became conscious of the fact after a while that he was still clutching the bloody knife in his right hand, and he wiped the knife on a tuft of grass before putting it back into his belt.

He had no fear of other Utes in the vicinity at this time. The Utes would not come looking for him in the night even if they'd heard the shots. But tomorrow, this canyon would become a hornet's nest, which meant that he had to be far from it.

The horses were gone. It would have taken days to round up this loose bunch, and he had less than twenty-four hours to get out of these mountains.

He got up, then, and he walked north, and in less than five minutes he found the gray, a dim, ghostly shadow in the darkness. He rode back down the canyon, passing the body of the Indian he'd killed with the knife, seeing the moonlight glowing on the bronzed, still features and the staring eyes.

The Ute wore a silver medallion which may have been taken from the body of a dead padre who'd penetrated these mountains. The medallion had not brought the Ute the luck he'd thought it would.

Grady Mulvane glanced back when he was twenty-five yards from the dead Indian, and he could still see the moon shining on the medallion around the Ute's neck.

CHAPTER
TWO

Two weeks later Grady stood on the porch of the Cheyenne Saloon in a town which went by the name of Bottle Springs. A cold rain leaked down out of the black night sky, and Grady watched it splash on the worn wooden boardwalk in front of him, illuminated by the yellow light from the batwing doors of the saloon.

He had reached this place ten minutes ago, and he'd put up the gray at a nearby stable, giving the hostler the last few coins he'd had in his pockets to feed and rub down the animal.

He would have liked to push up to the bar and have a drink or two to warm the inside of him — it had been wet riding all through the day — but he missed tobacco more than liquor. His tobacco had run out on him two days after leaving the canyon in which he'd killed the three Utes, and there had been no chance of replenishing his store.

He'd eaten well on the way east from the mountains because game had been plentiful, a mule-tailed deer on one occasion, and then a buffalo cow a few days later. He'd carried the buffalo meat all the way to Bottle Springs, having had his last meal only a mile or two out on the plains after having raised the lights of the town.

He didn't know this town, because he was considerably south of his usual haunts, but it had been the first town he'd struck since coming out of the mountains. He had been pushing aimlessly east, not particularly caring where he came out.

His little stake which he'd put into this wild-horse venture was gone, and he had to get another one. There were always ranchers in this part of the country who would be taking on extra hands, especially a man who could break horses, even though this job he didn't relish. He'd seen too many stove-in cowpunchers, their insides ruined by the bucking of hammerhead horses.

A man in black, flat-crowned hat and brown leather vest had come out of a building across the way, and was now crossing the muddy street, picking his way carefully to avoid the biggest puddles, and as he came Grady caught a glimpse of a silver star on his shirt.

This was the law of Bottle Springs, not a big town, not a small town, two parallel streets with a connecting side street, and only one of the parallel streets was worth mentioning because it had a dozen or so saloons, and a stage office, and as Grady had ridden in minutes before he'd seen the stage getting ready to pull out — six horses steaming in the wet rain as they waited, and the mail bags were loaded into the front and rear boots.

He'd passed a small stage yard, too, where several Concords stood in line, obviously in need of repair, one of them with the front wheels off and up on jacks. This town, then, was the headquarters for a small stage line which operated in the area.

Grady considered the possibilities of working for a stage line. He'd ridden shotgun messenger for a line far toward the north, and on a few occasions he'd even handled the three spans of horses, always a tricky assignment. There were always plenty of jobs around a stage headquarters — in the yard, wheelwrights, carpenters, joiners, hostlers, yard men — and then plenty more along the line at the various swing and home stations. Seeing the stage yard, Grady was positive he'd come to the right place.

The lawman who had been crossing the street came up on the walk directly in front of Grady, and then headed for the three steps which led up to the porch. He was a big man with sandy hair and a blunt nose, and a kind of fixed smile on his face.

The gun on his hip was a pearl-handled Colt Peacemaker, and he looked like a man who would know how to use it. As he came up the steps he gave Grady a thorough inspection, and Grady said to him sourly, "Take a good look, mister."

"My business." The lawman smiled.

Grady Mulvane knew what he looked like without the aid of a mirror. He'd been on the move for the past two weeks, and all through the summer, living out in the hills and never going near a town, and neither he nor Joe Beauford had paid too much attention to their appearance. He was seedy now, and down at the heels. To a stranger he would be just another saddlebum looking for a handout, his pockets empty.

The amusing thought suddenly struck him that this was about what he was. Until that band of mountain

14

Utes had ridden out of the hills, however, he'd stood a fair chance of amounting to something. Now he had to start from scratch again.

The lawman had pulled up and was standing on the porch now, rubbing his back against one of the porch pillars as he looked at Grady.

"Just ride in?" he asked.

"You know it," Grady told him.

It was this man's business to know who was new in this town. He was only making talk now, sizing up his man.

"Riding through?" the sheriff of Bottle Springs asked.

Grady looked at him. "You ask a hell of a lot of questions," he said.

The big man smiled. "You got any reason for not answering them?" he asked softly.

Grady scowled at the rain beating down on the walk. "Reckon I'll take a job, if there is one," he said.

He'd put it on the line, then, that he wasn't a bum, and he wouldn't be riding through, and didn't have a posse on his tail. This was what had been in the back of the sheriff's mind.

"Name's Champion," the sandy-haired man said. "Ben Champion. You're in Bottle Springs, mister, and I'm its sheriff. You look like you could stand a drink, and it's on me."

Grady nodded briefly and turned to follow the sheriff into the saloon. He said, as they pushed in through the doors, "Next one's on me, when I get a job."

"Remember it," Ben Champion nodded.

15

They walked past several card tables toward the bar, and a number of men nodded to the sheriff and eyed Grady reflectively.

"You buy drinks for every drifter comes through this way?" Grady asked as they pulled up at the bar.

"You're not a drifter," Champion said easily.

"How would you know?"

"Reckon I've met my share of drifters." The sheriff smiled.

He had blue eyes to go with that sandy hair, and the eyes were level. Looking at him in the bar mirror, Grady felt himself liking the man. Ben Champion was not patronizing. This night he was simply buying a drink for a man who momentarily was down on his luck, and he expected Grady to return the compliment when he was back in the chips.

A bartender came toward them, and without a word took down a bottle from the shelf and pushed it toward the sheriff, along with two glasses. Then he eyed Grady narrowly and said, "Wet night, Ben."

"It's wet," Ben Champion agreed.

As he was pouring the drinks, Grady said to him, "What's your trouble in this town?"

Champion grinned. "You're sharp," he said. "How would you know?"

"People don't give a saddlebum this much attention," Grady observed.

"Reckon you're making sense," the sheriff nodded. "Keep on it."

Grady downed his drink, feeling the warmth of the liquor go through his body.

16

"You have a stage line in this town," he observed. "I'd say somebody's been breaking into those Wells Fargo boxes."

Ben Champion's grin broadened. "It wasn't you," he said. "Some of this crowd here may have gotten that idea. Every stranger rides in now is looked at with suspicion."

"How do you know it wasn't me?" Grady asked him idly.

"You'd have the price of a drink," Champion said, "and you wouldn't be standing out there in the cold. That bunch working on Jim Lamonte's stages have done pretty well lately."

Grady nodded thoughtfully, and he watched Champion push the bottle toward him.

"Hit it again," the sheriff said, "and that'll be it. You'll owe me two when you get your job."

"What job?" Grady asked him.

Ben Champion rubbed his jaw. "Stage line's always hiring men," he said. "I'll talk to Jim Lamonte. Who will I say wants the job?"

"Grady Mulvane," Grady said. "I'm known up in the Bow Ridge country."

Ben Champion whistled. "You're far from home, Mulvane," he said.

Grady told him about their summer rounding up wild horses, and then of the Ute raid on their camp.

"Stripped you clean," Champion said sympathetically. "Some of those tribes back in the mountains are bad. They get off scot free?"

"Three of them didn't," Grady told him, and he saw the respect come into the big man's eyes.

Ben Champion paid for the drinks, and then he said, "You haven't got a bed for tonight, there's always a cot over at the jailhouse across the way. Make yourself at home."

"I'm obliged," Grady smiled. "Reckon I'll have to take you up."

"You eaten?"

"Wild meat all the way in," Grady told him. "I'm all right."

"Let you know if Jim Lamonte's in his office," Champion said. "He might be able to fix something up for you tonight, yet."

Grady nodded his thanks again, and he watched the sheriff move toward the batwing doors and the street. It was about eight o'clock in the evening, and a man wearing the star would begin making his rounds of the town about now.

It was an indication of the man's character, too. Grady had known many lawmen who on a damp night like this would have been content to sit in at one of the card games in a warm saloon, letting the trouble come to them if there was any. Ben Champion intended to make his usual rounds.

Pushing away from the bar, Grady headed for a vacant table near the far wall. The Cheyenne Saloon was not particularly crowded this mid-week night. He imagined that the majority of men present were stage hands, yard men, possibly a driver or two, or hostlers. There were riders from some of the nearby ranches,

18

also, and some passengers from back east who'd evidently stopped over in Bottle Springs for the night.

There was a greasy deck of cards on the table, and Grady picked them up and started to shuffle through them idly, conscious of the fact that many men in this place were still wondering about him. Ordinarily, a drifter was one thing, and every town had plenty of them, but a drifter in a town which had been having a series of stage holdups was another thing. Grady thumbed through the cards, and then set them down on the table solitaire fashion, and he had the first row out in front of him when he saw a man step up and stop by the table.

"Had your free drink," the man said, "and now you're here for the night. That it, mister?"

Grady looked up at him. He'd noticed this man at the far end of the bar when he'd come in. He was a big fellow with heavy shoulders, the left one carried slightly higher than the right. He had peppery hair to go with a freckled face and tough blue-green eyes.

Grady looked at his hands because the hands usually told what a man did for a living. This blocky man's hands were square, solid, but not particularly calloused. He could have been a stage driver, for these men were careful of their hands, always wearing expensive, fleece-lined gloves.

"What's your trouble?" Grady asked softly.

"Reckon I don't like drifters," the blocky man told him.

"You own this establishment?" Grady wanted to know.

"Hell with that," the man scowled. "I don't like bums comin' in here for free drinks, an' then makin' themselves at home."

Grady looked at him. "Go back to the bar where you came from," he advised.

He saw the red come into the man's face, and he knew then that he had his fight, and he found some small pleasure in this because he still wasn't over that Ute raid and Joe Beauford's death. He still wanted to smash out at something, anything, and for two weeks he'd been just running, knowing that avenging Ute war parties could be fairly close by.

"I don't take that talk from a bum," the blocky man said evenly.

"You'll take it from me," Grady said.

He was looking down at the cards as he continued to lay them out on the table, conscious of the fact that all talk had stopped in the Cheyenne, and that men were watching them, calculating who would make the first move.

"Let him alone, Ed," a man called from the other end of the room.

There was no authority in the request. This was just an acquaintance of Ed's who didn't think Ed ought to bother with a nobody.

"Keep at it, Ed," Grady said. "You're in pretty far now."

He was going to fight a bigger, heavier man in a few moments, and undoubtedly the friend of Ed's had considered that. Grady Mulvane looked thin and run down, but this was deceiving, the deception being partly made up by the worn-out clothes he was wearing.

Underneath the broken-at-the-seams coat were whipcord muscles. He'd wielded an axe and a sledgehammer a good part of this summer, making that big V-shaped corral for the mustangs, and he'd broken plenty of wild horses.

There was not an ounce of surplus flesh on his lean body, but it was the fire which burned inside of him, and which had been lit by the savage killing of Joe Beauford, which made him a hundred times more dangerous.

That fire would not go out. The killing of the Ute with his knife had helped, but Grady Mulvane needed something else. He needed to smash at something, at someone, with his bare fists, and keep smashing and smashing until the fire was quenched, and now Ed had gone out of his way asking for this, pushing for it.

Ed said, "Get up on your feet, bum."

Grady Mulvane straightened the packet of cards in his hands, and then placed them on the top of the table. He rubbed his unshaven face with his right hand and said softly, "You got yourself a fight, mister."

CHAPTER
THREE

The bartender who had waited on Grady and Ben Champion said morosely from the other end of the bar, "Why don't you take it outside, Grubaker."

"Wet outside," Ed Grubaker smiled.

He was watching Grady closely, a sheen in his eyes and a smile on his face. This was a man who liked to hurt another man, and this to him was a fight where the other man would be hurt. He'd sized up Grady from the bar, and he'd thought he was safe in picking his fight.

Grady was standing up now, and the two men looked at each other across the table. Still a small provocation was needed, and Grady provided it without hesitation. Ed Grubaker had done his share, and now Grady felt that he had to assume some of the responsibility for this affair. Grasping the edge of the table with both ends, he shoved the table forward, not hard, but sufficient to unbalance Grubaker.

Grubaker stumbled a little and came back swinging a heavy fist across the table, cursing as he did so. He missed with the punch because Grady pulled his body back, and then Grady rammed the table forward hard this time, the edge of it catching Grubaker across the front, knocking him back, and Grady went over the table as it overturned like a big panther, slashing at his man with both hands. The men at the nearest card table scrambled to their feet and got out of the way as the two men hit the floor, rolling under the table, upsetting this one, too, and spilling liquor, cards and chips over the floor.

Grady was hitting out at his man savagely even as they scrambled to their feet, and he saw the doubt come into Grubaker's green eyes. Grubaker had had his fights before, but he'd never fought with a savage animal, and he was not so sure of himself now.

He was strong, though, and he was not a quitter, and he knew his way around in a rough-and-tumble fight. When Grady charged at him, he brought up his right knee, seeking to drive it into Grady's groin, but Grady anticipated the move, swinging his body away and then smashing his left fist deep into Grubaker's stomach.

As Grubaker stumbled back, grasping for air, Grady tore after him, the fire burning fiercely inside him now. He could not see Grubaker clearly, because there was a film of hate across his eyes, but he could smash at him, and he smashed with both fists, driving his man before him, hitting at the body, at the face, smashing at Grubaker's weakening arms, punching and moving forward.

He heard a man yell, "They better stop that!"

He had Grubaker back against the bar now, and he was still slashing at him, scarcely conscious of the fact that Grubaker's arms had now fallen at his sides, and he was a helpless wreck of a man, blood streaming from his battered face.

Then the roof fell on Grady Mulvane's head. There was an explosion inside his head, and the floor came up at him very fast, striking him on the side of the face. Even as the darkness closed over him he could see Ed Grubaker sliding to a sitting position against the bar in front of him, his face hideous with blood, beaten out of shape in these few fierce moments of fighting.

When Grady's dark eyes started to function again, he found himself looking up at a whitewashed ceiling, and he was lying on a hard cot. Someone had been placing damp cloths on his face to revive him, and the cloth was just coming away when his eyes opened.

He could hear the rain outside the window above the cot, and the window had iron bars on it, and he suspected now where he was. The man sitting on a stool beside him and using the wet cloth was Ben Champion, and Champion said casually, "Head feel big?"

"Big as a balloon," Grady scowled. He felt the pain running down the back of his neck when he lifted his head slightly to look around. He was in one of the cells of the Bottle Springs jailhouse, a narrow cubicle of a room with brick walls and an iron-barred front. "Who hit me?" he asked.

"I did," Champion said. "You would have killed Grubaker, otherwise."

Grady looked at him sourly. "What the hell did you use?" he asked, "a brick bat?"

"Barrel of my gun," Champion smiled. "I've learned how to use just enough force to stop a thing like that."

"You stopped it," Grady told him grimly. "They must have harder heads than mine in this part of the country."

"You didn't want to kill a man," Champion said.

Grady shook his head. "I didn't want to kill him," he agreed. "I'm obliged to you for the rap on the head."

"I didn't hear the whole thing," Champion went on. "Grubaker push you? He generally does go after smaller men."

"He pushed me." Grady nodded.

The sheriff of Bottle Springs looked down at him quizzically. "Reckon you kind of hoped he would."

Grady stared up at the ceiling, conscious of the fact for the first time that the fire was out inside of him. He was a normal, rational man again, and Joe Beauford could rest in his shallow grave in the foothills of the Rockies.

"I'm glad he pushed me," he said. "Who is Grubaker?"

"Drives for Lamonte Line," Champion told him. "Never liked him, myself, but he's never given me any trouble."

"You're wearing a tin star," Grady observed. "I wasn't tonight, and I wasn't shaved, and I looked as if I just crawled out of a stable loft."

Champion smiled. "I'll take off that star for any man in this town," he said, and Grady Mulvane believed him. "When you're feeling up to it," Champion went on, "we'll take a walk up to Lamonte Line office. Jim says he'll talk to you."

"Tonight?"

"Why not tonight? You can use a job right away."

Grady sat up on the cot, had another dizzy spell, and waited until it went away. "Next time," he said, "tell me when you want me to stop fighting."

"You wouldn't have listened," Champion smiled. "You don't talk to a mountain lion clawing a helpless old cow."

Grady got up and walked around the room a few times. Then he buttoned his coat. Ben Champion took a cigar from his coat pocket and tucked it between Grady's teeth.

"That's for the belt on the head," he said. "Ready to go?"

They left the jailhouse and walked south on the main street until they came to the stage depot. The evening stage had been leaving when Grady came into town, and the depot was empty now except for a man with a green eyeshade who stood behind a caged window going over some books.

"Office in the back," Champion said. He nodded to the clerk at the window and he said, "Back again, Lou."

The clerk looked Grady over carefully under the eyeshade, but said nothing.

Ben Champion paused at a door which led to the inner office, and he knocked. A man said, "All right, Ben."

The sheriff pushed through the door, nodding for Grady to follow him.

26

Grady walked in after him, expecting to find a lone man in the office, and he found himself looking into the dark violet eyes of the most beautiful woman he'd ever encountered in his twenty-seven years of living.

She had been pouring coffee into a cup at the desk of the thin, white-faced man in black who sat there before a sheaf of papers, and she looked up when they came in.

"Judith," Ben Champion murmured, taking off his hat. "I didn't think you were here."

"Thought I'd bring Jim a pot of coffee." The girl smiled. "He told me you were coming back."

Brady had managed to get the broken-brimmed hat from his head, but he was still staring at the girl at the desk. She could have been twenty-one or two, and she had dark hair drawn in a bunch at the back. The face was perfectly formed, with an exquisite nose and mouth, and a warmth in her smile.

Champion said, "Jim, Grady Mulvane. And Mr. Lamonte's sister, Judith."

"How are you, Mr. Mulvane," Judith said, and for the first time Grady realized what he looked like, and he felt the shame of it.

Ben Champion seemed to realize this, too, in some embarrassment, and he said quickly, addressing the thin-faced man at the desk, "I told you Grady was down on his luck, Jim. Ute's stripped him of his gear and killed his partner back in the mountains. He's been rounding up wild horses all summer."

Jim Lamonte nodded. He had his sister's violet eyes, and he could have been ten or fifteen years older. There were hollows in his cheeks and his hands were long and slender — the hands of a woman.

"Tough break, Mulvane," Lamonte said.

"Would you gentlemen like coffee?" Judith asked. "There's plenty to go around."

"Reckon I wouldn't mind," Ben Champion murmured, and glancing at him Grady could see how it was with this man. The sheriff of Bottle Springs was in love with the girl, and for some reason Grady Mulvane did not welcome this knowledge.

He watched Judith Lamonte get two cups from a cupboard in the corner, and then pour the coffee. He stood there with his broken hat in his hand, and he cursed the Utes for stealing his razor.

Jim Lamonte was saying, "You've worked a lot with horses, Mulvane?"

"Plenty," Grady said. "Broken them, handled them, even shoed them."

"We need a station man at one of our swing stations," Lamonte said. "First swing station out of Bottle Springs. We keep two men at the station to handle the stock and make the changes. One man walked out on us."

"What station is that?" Ben Champion asked as he picked up his coffee cup.

"Elder Creek," Lamonte told him. He said to Grady, "It's not like being stuck out in the desert somewhere. You're only twelve miles from Bottle Springs. The pay is forty a month and keep."

"I'll take it," Grady said.

Judith Lamonte smiled up at him as she pushed a cup of the hot coffee in his direction.

"I'm obliged," Grady said.

"You look as if you can stand it," she said, and she gave him another smile. Then she put the empty pot on a tray and she said, "You men will want to talk. Please excuse me."

"I can't walk you home." Ben Champion smiled. "My hard luck."

"We could move farther out in the country." Judith laughed. "But I think Jim prefers living next to the stage office."

"Convenient," Jim Lamonte said. He put a cigar in his mouth and touched a match to it as his sister left, Ben Champion holding the door open for her. "Can you go out to Elder Springs with the morning stage?" Lamonte asked Grady when the door closed behind his sister.

"Sooner the better," Grady told him.

Lamonte opened a drawer, and then a metal cash box. He slipped a few bills from it and shoved them toward Grady.

"There's a month's salary in advance," he said. "You look as if you could use it."

Grady looked down at the money. "Suppose I take it and skip," he said.

Jim Lamonte looked over at Ben Champion.

"He won't skip," Ben smiled.

"I didn't think you'd have brought him around otherwise," Lamonte observed. "You'll be working with

Tom O'Hara, Mulvane. He's an easy man to get along with."

"Ed Grubaker wasn't." Ben Champion grinned, and Jim Lamonte looked at him curiously. "Your new station man damn near took Grubaker apart tonight in the Cheyenne Saloon," Champion went on. "Reckon it'll be a week before Ed's able to handle a team for you, Jim."

Jim Lamonte looked at Grady again. "A fighter," he said.

"Grubaker pushed it," Ben told him, "and he's had it coming to him one hell of a long time."

"Take your word for that, too, Ben," Lamonte nodded. "I don't like brawlers on my line, Mulvane. You can understand that."

Grady nodded. "One thing more," he said. He'd picked up the money and pocketed it, and he was ready to go.

"What is it?" Lamonte asked.

"Hear your stages have been getting hit," Grady told him. "Anything I can do to help?"

"Keep your eyes open," Lamonte said. "Not too much a station man can do. Just hang on to your horses."

"They haven't hit at the horses as yet," Ben Champion pointed out. "They've been after cash in the Wells Fargo boxes."

"Whatever they take," Lamonte said gloomily, "it's always bad for the line. People don't like to ride a line which is being hit like this."

"That Wells Fargo man come out yet?" Champion asked him.

"Due any day," Lamonte said.

"Seen them work before," Ben smiled. "They nose around, ask questions, ride here and ride there, and the holdups break out again when they're gone."

"Wells Fargo threaten to stop shipments?" Grady asked.

"They always do," Lamonte said, "but they're in a hole, too. This is the only stage line operating in this section of the territory. They don't ship by us, they don't ship at all. That's why they're sending a man out."

Grady listened to this conversation as he sipped the hot coffee Judith Lamonte had poured for him. He understood the situation as far as Wells Fargo was concerned. The big express company moved cash and bullion over its own lines, and over the smaller connecting lines where it was not established, and some of the smaller lines, like Lamonte Line, would depend upon this subsidy for its existence. Wells Fargo, on the other hand, expected its shipments to go through, and when road agents hit too hard and too often, they put a lot of pressure upon the line over which they were shipping.

"How many holdups have you had?" Grady asked.

"Four or five," Lamonte said. "None of them real big, but it could happen any time."

"Anybody killed?"

"Not yet," Ben Champion murmured. "It'll come to that. Jim has shotgun messengers riding the seat now."

Grady learned more about Lamonte Line before he left the stage office that night. Jim Lamonte had bought the line two years before, and was struggling to put it on its feet financially. It was not big. Lamonte Line had a three-hundred-mile run from Bottle Springs down to Sherman City. There were about twenty stations strung out along the run. Some of them were home stations where the passengers could get meals, and stop over if they so desired; most were swing stations, such as the one at Elder Creek where Grady would be going, designed only to swing fresh horses into the traces, and keep the stages moving at a fast rate of speed.

Leaving with Ben Champion and walking down in the direction of the Bottle Springs Hotel where Grady had decided to take a room for the night, Grady said to the sheriff, "Lamonte's having a rough time running his line. He know his business?"

Champion frowned. "If Jim Lamonte came to me now for advice as to his buying a stage line, I'd tell him no. It takes the combination of a pretty good man and a great deal of luck these days to run a line in the black."

"Seems like a good man," Grady observed.

"He is a good man," Champion nodded. "Maybe not a good stage line man, but a good man."

"And he'll go broke?"

Ben Champion shrugged. "We'll see," he said. "Maybe the Wells Fargo man will be able to break this thing up."

"You've had no luck?" Grady asked him.

"Looked around," Champion admitted. "Most of these holdups have taken place fifty or a hundred miles down the line, out of my jurisdiction, but I've looked around."

"Nine times out of ten," Grady observed, "these things begin pretty close to home. Takes somebody who knows which stages will be carrying the big hauls. That means somebody in Bottle Springs."

"Figured that," Champion nodded. "They're playing it pretty close to the vest." They walked on, and when they came to the front of the hotel Champion stopped. "You'll be in town now and then," he said. "You know where my office is. Keep your eyes and ears open out at Elder Creek. You might hear something."

"Reckon I'd like to break this up," Grady said thoughtfully.

Ben Champion looked at him. "For Jim Lamonte?" he asked.

"Why not?" Grady countered, knowing what Champion was driving at. "He gave me a job."

"What do you think of his sister?"

"I noticed," Grady said gravely, "that you think a lot of her."

Champion laughed aloud. "We're not engaged," he said, "if that's what you're fishing around for. She's still fair game."

"But you wouldn't like it if I tried to cut in on you."

"I couldn't stop you," Champion told him.

"No," Grady Mulvane said, "you couldn't stop me."

He wondered why it had to be this way. He liked Ben Champion, who was a square shooter, and Ben apparently was very much in love with the first girl Grady had ever looked at twice, and wanted to look at again. It was the way the cards fell out, and it was not a good way.

CHAPTER
FOUR

In the morning, Grady had plenty of time to get his hair cut and have the whiskers shaved from his face. He also picked up a clean shirt and a pair of levis, and a hat to replace the battered one he'd worn into Bottle Springs the previous night.

Buying a few odds and ends he'd have to take out with him to Elder Creek, and paying his hotel bill, and his breakfast, left him almost where he'd been the night before, but he no longer looked like a trail bum looking for a handout.

He had to make a decision about the gelding. Working for Lamonte Line, he now had the privilege of using Lamonte stock; he wouldn't really need the gray any more, but the big horse had served him well for a number of years, and he decided to take it out with him to Elder Creek.

With the morning stage due in at ten o'clock, Grady was out in front of the stage office with plenty of time to spare. A Concord was already being prepared in the yard of Lamonte Line, and the big coach rolled out in front of the depot ten minutes before the westbound Great Western Line coach was due.

Great Western had its last stop in Bottle Springs, and here Lamonte Line took over, transferring passengers, mail, and the Wells Fargo box to its own coach for the run to Sherman City.

The driver who sat up on the box of the Lamonte coach looked at Grady as he came up leading the gray gelding. Then he spat and said, "Hell of a fight last night, mister."

"How's Grubaker?" Grady asked him.

"Both eyes shut," the driver grinned, "an' he ain't feelin' good yet. I'm takin' his run today. You done him up right."

Grady didn't say anything to this. He tied the gray to the back of the coach, the driver watching him curiously, and then he said, "Signed up last night with Lamonte. You'll drop me off at Elder Creek station."

The driver's eyes widened. "Ed Grubaker will be damned pleased to hear that," he murmured.

Grady shrugged. He knew he'd made a bad enemy in Grubaker, and that he would have to be on his guard, but he wasn't particularly worried about the man. He stood on the walk examining the horses in the traces, matched chestnuts, and good stock, and then he said to the driver, "The road agents ever bother you?"

"Not yet," the man said. He was a short, stubby chap with reddish hair and a flattened nose. "They hit Grubaker twice, but not me."

"Grubaker," Grady said thoughtfully.

He heard light steps coming toward him on the walk, then, and turning, he saw Judith Lamonte coming up. She was wearing a fetching blue dress with white ruffles at the collar and on the sleeves. Hatless, her dark hair gleamed in the morning sunshine, which seemed exceptionally bright after the rain of the previous night.

Grady touched his new hat to her, and she slowed down, looking at him curiously. She didn't recognize him, shaved, and with new clothes, and he said by way of explanation, "New station man out at Elder Creek. You gave me coffee last night."

"Mr. Mulvane," she said, surprised.

"I'd been roughing it for two weeks," Grady apologized. "The Utes took my razor."

"I meant to tell you how sorry I was for your misfortune."

"The way the cards fall out," Grady said.

He noticed in the sunlight that her eyes were a shade lighter in color than he'd thought, and there were a few small freckles on her nose. This was a fine, warm-hearted girl, but Ben Champion had been here first.

"We're glad to have you with Lamonte Line," Judith said, and the way she said it, she meant it.

Grady watched her go into the office, and for the moment he wished Jim Lamonte had been able to give him employment in town.

The stage driver said, "There's a real gal, mister."

Grady didn't have to be told that.

The Great Western coach was coming in at the far end of town, and Grady watched as it rolled to a stop in the alley next to the Lamonte depot. A rider sat up on the box with the driver, shotgun in the holster on the side of the seat. Four weary passengers, who'd probably ridden all night, got out of the coach and stumbled across the road to the restaurant for a quick breakfast before pushing on.

Two men came out of the Lamonte depot to unbolt the Wells Fargo chest from the floor of the coach box, and then carry it to the waiting Lamonte stage. They looked at Grady suspiciously as they bolted it to the floor below the driver's seat, and the driver said casually, "New man goin' out to Elder Creek Station. Mr. Lamonte signed him up last night."

Jim Lamonte, himself, came out of the office a few minutes later, looked at Grady in approval, and said, "You look better. Keep the stock in shape out at Elder Creek."

"Do my best," Grady nodded.

Jim Lamonte had put him on his feet, and he appreciated this. If there was any way in which he could help Lamonte, he intended to do it. According to Ben Champion, Lamonte's main problem now was to stop the raids on his coaches.

Lamonte spoke to the driver, and then stepped away from the coach to look up the street. In a few moments a man came hurrying out of the China Doll Saloon, wiping his mouth on his sleeve.

He was a lanky man with a long neck and a hang-dog expression on his face. He'd already had a few drinks this early in the morning, which would automatically disqualify him as a shotgun messenger in Grady's opinion, but the lanky man nodded to Jim Lamonte and then climbed up on the seat beside the driver.

Grady glanced at the stage line owner, thinking he would have noticed that his employee would never be able to keep a man in the sights of his shotgun if he had to.

Lamonte seemed to have taken no notice of the fact that the messenger had just come out of a saloon at an early hour in the morning.

Lamonte said, "Good trip."

Then he went back into the office, and Grady Mulvane was thinking that Lamonte Line would never prosper with an owner who'd overlook drunkenness on the part of a man who was riding the stage to protect it. Possibly, Lamonte hadn't been aware of the fact that his messenger was not in good shape. It was probably closer to the truth, though, that Lamonte was the kind of man who didn't like to make trouble for anyone, and he was assuming that his messenger would straighten out on the road.

It was a loose way to run a stage line, though, and Grady felt the resentment rising in him as he watched the lanky man up on the box. He was sure that once they were out of sight of Bottle Springs, the messenger would be curled up on the mailbags on the roof. If trouble came he'd put his hands up and let it go at that.

The passengers were coming out of the restaurant now, climbing back inside. Grady deliberated for a moment, wondering whether he ought to ride up on the roof, inside the coach, or on the gelding. He decided to go up on the roof so that he could have a few words with driver and messenger.

When he climbed up, the lanky man stared at him suspiciously, spat, and said to the driver, "Who the hell is this, Barney?"

Grady settled back against the mailbags and stared at the man steadily. He said softly, "I could be the special agent sent out by Wells Fargo, and what the hell would you do about it?"

The lanky man had no answer to this, but he didn't like the remark, and his neck reddened. He said to Barney, "He ain't Wells Fargo?"

Barney grinned as he kicked the brake loose and shook the three teams out into the road. "You heard of the lickin' Ed Grubaker took last night?"

"Heard it," the lanky man muttered.

"Him," Barney said, jerking his head back toward Grady, who was reclining against the piled-up mailbags, facing the backs of the two men on the box. "We're takin' him out to Elder Creek. Station man."

"I still could be Wells Fargo," Grady observed.

"You could," Barney nodded, "but I don't figure you are, mister. Never seen a Wells Fargo man who'd get himself dirtied up the way you did last night. How about that, Buck?"

Buck turned to glare at Grady. "You're the funny one, mister," he said.

Grady smiled at him. "You always ride the box with two or three in you, Buck?" he asked.

"Any of your damned business?" Buck snarled, turning to face Grady completely now.

"Reckon I'm on the Lamonte payroll," Grady said. "Might mean something."

"Not to me," Buck snapped.

"Easy with him," Barney warned. "He's a damned wildcat, Buck."

"Kind of rough, myself," Buck scowled, but he no longer was as nasty as he'd been, and he was remembering what had happened to Grubaker.

Grady said nothing. He sat there against the mailbags, arms folded, a smile on his face. He knew, and Buck knew, and Barney knew, that Buck was edging away from it now. Drink had made him a little reckless, but he was remembering now.

"If I ran Lamonte Line," Grady told him, "I'd dump you at Elder Creek, and you'd walk back to town. Might take some of the liquor out of you."

"You ain't runnin' Lamonte Line," Buck growled. He would have liked to say more, but he didn't, and Grady let it rest there. He'd pushed his man hard enough; he could have pushed him a lot harder, and Buck still would have backed away from it, but there was no sense to it, and he didn't like to ride a man just for the sake of riding him . . .

The heavy Concord coach rolled west, the six chestnuts moving nicely in the traces. Grady leaned back against the mail sacks and looked up at the sky, and he found his mind going back again and again to Judith Lamonte. He knew that it was foolishness, and that Ben Champion had the inside track and undoubtedly deserved it, but Miss Lamonte's smile and her warmth had attracted him, and he was going to have a time getting her off his mind.

The run out to Elder Creek station was a short one, but there was a good grade going up over a ridge known as Dutchman's Ridge, and on the other side Barney Weston let the chestnuts run, and they were breathing hard as they pulled into the yard of Elder Creek.

Three teams of horses were waiting for them, and a thin-faced gray-haired man in battered felt hat was standing outside the stone corral, waiting to take the chestnuts out of the traces and walk the new teams in. The old man would be Tom O'Hara, who was to help Grady run Elder Creek. Lamonte had assured him that he would have no trouble with old Tom, who knew stock.

The swing station consisted of the corral, a part-stone, part-sod, and part-timber house with a stone chimney, a shed in the rear which could accommodate as much as a dozen horses in inclement weather, and another smaller building which seemed to be unoccupied, and may have been the original station years before.

The coach had to swing across a small wooden bridge over a creek which was lined with willows, and which twisted out across miles of barren country, most of it treeless, this green snake of Elder Creek apparently the only living thing. The stage road beyond the creek paralleled the creek for some distance, and then turned south as the creek followed a more westerly direction.

Barney Weston said to Grady as he pulled up his teams, "Last stop, Mulvane. Old Tom here ain't the talkin' kind, but he's a good man."

Grady climbed down from the coach, leaving Buck Neil, the messenger, still up on the box, glowering down at him, saying nothing in parting.

The passengers stepped out, also, to stretch their legs, and Grady went to the rear boot to untie the gray.

Barney Weston said to the old man, "Tom, this here's Grady Mulvane, come out to run Elder Creek station."

Tom O'Hara looked at Grady under grizzled eyebrows. His eyes were clear and blue, the eyes of a much younger man. He shook hands briefly and said, "Hear you give Ed Grubaker hell last night."

"News travels in this country," Grady murmured.

"Rider come through an hour ago," O'Hara told him. "Grubaker had it comin' to him. Welcome to Elder Creek, what the hell there is of it."

He looked around at this tiny oasis, a few trees, the creek, the buildings, and the corral, and then the endless spaces rolling back up to Dutchman's Ridge, and then on out east, west, south.

Grady grinned and said, "Reckon I didn't come out here to look at the scenery."

"It don't bother me," O'Hara told him. "Soon look at this as them damn fools back in town."

This was the ideal man, Grady realized, for station attendant. O'Hara was the natural loner. He preferred his own company, or the company of one or two men, to that of several hundred in a town.

Grady wasn't built that way, himself, and this Elder Creek job was something temporary. A man could save money out here, because there was no way to spend it. In a year's time or less he would be able to get into something more to his liking. He didn't know what that was as yet, but he wasn't going to live his life out at a place like Elder Creek. Possibly the stage line was the answer to his problem. He knew horses, and horses made the line go. He felt that he could keep a tighter rein on men than Jim Lamonte did, too, and that had its importance.

Tom O'Hara got the fresh stock into the traces, turning the six horses Barney Weston had brought into the stone corral. The passengers got back inside, and Weston kicked his brake loose.

Grady nodded to the driver's cheery grin, but Buck Neil stared straight ahead of him, his eyes stony. When the Concord had rumbled down the road, Tom O'Hara said, "What in hell's wrong with Neil?"

"We had a few words," Grady admitted. "Jim Lamonte permit his men to drink while they're on duty?"

O'Hara looked at him. "Lamonte permits a hell of a lot that another stage owner wouldn't permit," he said. "Reckon you heard that back in town."

"Finding it out," Grady murmured. "He doesn't run a tight line."

"It ain't tight," O'Hara admitted. "Lamonte's a good man, but not a good stage man." He glanced at Grady and he said, "You met his sister?"

"Yes." Grady nodded. He was watching the Concord move across the flat to the west, dust broiling up behind it.

"Ben Champion's got his halter on that one," O'Hara said, and he was still watching Grady.

44

"There's a good man," Grady said.

"Everybody's good," O'Hara growled, "an' still the damn Lamonte stages are bein' held up. Lamonte's got six months more the way his line's goin'."

Grady stared at the older man. "As bad as that?"

"That's the talk," O'Hara told him. "You don't run a stage line unless you got Well Fargo express on it, an' the United States mail. You lose both of 'em, an' you're dead. The way it's goin' Lamonte's losing both of 'em."

"This Wells Fargo man coming out might stop it," Grady pointed out.

O'Hara laughed tonelessly. "He might end up with a bullet in the back, too," he said. "This bunch ain't started throwin' lead as yet, but they will if it gets rough. The pickin's here are just too easy. They won't walk away from it because a Wells Fargo man turns up."

"Figured I'd look around, myself," Grady said. "I'll have time out here."

Tom O'Hara had some good advice for him, the advice of an old man who'd seen much of life, and was not too much impressed by it.

"Listen to me," he said. "You take care o' the stock, Grady. Let Lamonte worry about the holdups. You'll live a hell of a lot longer."

It was good advice, but Grady Mulvane was not too sure that he'd accept it.

CHAPTER
FIVE

The Wells Fargo man came through the next morning. He did not announce himself as such, but both Tom O'Hara and Grady spotted him immediately as he stepped down off the westbound coach to stretch his legs along with five other passengers.

He was a tall man, and he wore black, and he kept his coat buttoned because, Grady suspected, he kept a gun in an armpit holster under the left arm.

As he moved leisurely down along the corral wall, a cigar in his mouth, O'Hara said succinctly, "That's him, Grady."

Lamonte Line had him booked as just another passenger, which was the way Wells Fargo would want it, and the way Jim Lamonte would want it. The Wells Fargo man would make a leisurely inspection of the line as he rode from one end to the other, and then he might head back to Bottle Springs and take up residence there as a stock buyer, or a railroad man, or any occupation which would allay the suspicions that he was here to investigate stage holdups.

Without appearing to do so, the Wells Fargo special agent had his look around the station, gathered his own impressions of Tom O'Hara and Grady Mulvane, and said nothing at all.

In a matter of five minutes or less, Grady and O'Hara had changed the horses, and the stage was ready to roll again. The passengers got back inside, and they took off.

Tom O'Hara sat down on the corral wall and said, "He won't find nothin'. He'll ride out to Sherman City an' come back in three or four days, an' he'll find nothin'." He added significantly, "An' maybe he'll come back dead."

"He might know his business," Grady observed.

"This bunch knows his business, too," Tom scowled.

They had an equally interesting and more provocative passenger on the afternoon westbound, and Grady had to handle this one alone, as Tom O'Hara was out in the hills, looking for a bay horse which had broken out of the corral a few days before and headed for the open spaces.

Grady had his fresh teams ready when the coach came in, and for a few minutes he was busy making the changes. He did notice out of the corner of his eye that there were three passengers aboard this westbound, and one of them was a woman.

She was in traveling gray, and the two male passengers on the stage with her had evidently been competing for her attentions. One of them held the door open for her ceremoniously as she stepped down. The other asked her if he could get her a cup of cold water. Evidently, neither of them knew that she was remaining at Elder Creek.

It came as a shock to Grady Mulvane, also. He'd had a look at her as he went by with the third team of horses. She was not young, at least not a young girl. He figured her age to at least twenty-four or twenty-five.

She was not as tall as Judith Lamonte, nor nearly as beautiful, but a man would stop to look at her. With the second look you would see more than the first. She was the kind of woman who had to be looked at twice, or a man would dismiss her as just another woman.

Grady had only the first look at her as he went past with the leaders. She had nut-brown hair, and he thought her eyes were brown, too, but he could not be sure of this. Her mouth was rather wide, and firm. The lips were not as beautiful, nor as perfectly shaped as Judith Lamonte's, but it was a good mouth. The nose was straight, no tilt to it, and Grady liked this about her. She was fuller in the body than Judith, too, and there was more of the woman about her, possibly because she was a few years older.

When Grady had the three teams in the traces and ready to go, he noticed that the driver had taken the girl's bags down from the roof. There were two of them, and they were not new.

He was grinning as he said to Grady, "She's gettin' off here, Mulvane."

Grady stared at him. "Here?" he repeated.

At the home stations an occasional passenger would get off and rest up overnight, but the swing stations had no accommodations for passengers, especially female passengers.

48

"That's what her ticket says," the driver chuckled. "Gettin' off here, she tells me; supposed to meet somebody."

This evidently was news to the other two passengers, because they showed their disappointment as they reluctantly climbed back into the coach.

Grady stood to one side of the corral watching as the driver prepared to roll the Concord away. The situation was quite awkward, but yet the driver couldn't wait here until the party whom his passenger was to meet arrived. This was wide-open country, and a man could be delayed.

Grady found himself wondering idly who she was supposed to meet here. The woman was standing less than ten feet away from him, her two bags on the ground. She looked across at him, nodding slightly, and then she watched the coach move on, and Grady came over to pick up the bags.

"I'll put a chair over by the house in the shade," he said, and he picked up the bags. "Name's Mulvane. Grady Mulvane."

"Lorna Greene," she told him. "I'm obliged, Mr. Mulvane."

Another woman would have been embarrassed, even slightly apprehensive, at being left in this desolate place alone with a total stranger, but Lorna Greene seemed quite sure of herself. She looked at him steadily, and he saw then the hardness in her eyes, and he realized that this woman knew how to take care of herself in the presence of men. She'd had no trouble on the stage, and she'd have no trouble with him.

Grady walked on ahead of her with the bags, noticing that they were quite light. He heard her say behind him, "I'm to meet a Mr. Joseph Waddell at this place."

"This is Elder Creek station," Grady told her.

"That's the place," she said. "Do you know Mr. Waddell?"

"Came out here yesterday," Grady explained. "Reckon I'm new to this country, ma'am."

He hadn't heard Tom O'Hara mention anyone by the name of Waddell who lived in this vicinity. There were a few nesters up along the creek, but O'Hara hadn't mentioned anyone by name. Grady was thinking that it was highly irregular for a man to arrange to meet a woman at a place like this, and then not be here when she arrived. If Waddell lived here he would know that Elder Creek was not like the waiting room of the Lamonte Line in Bottle Springs.

Going into the shack, Grady came out with a chair and set it down outside under the shade of one of the cottonwoods.

"I am obliged," Lorna Greene said again as she sat down.

She'd had a cup of water, and Grady couldn't think of anything else he could do for her. He couldn't invite her into the house because a station man's shack was just that and nothing more.

He noticed that she was still very calm and detached as she sat down in the chair, straightening out her skirt. Grady leaned back against the wall of the shack and rolled a cigarette. He watched the Concord rolling down along the creek, and then he saw a rider moving along the road coming toward it. Rider and coach passed each other, and the rider came on in the direction of the station.

"Joe Waddell a relative?" Grady asked after a while.

She didn't answer right away, and when he looked over at her he noticed the slight, amused smile on her face.

"Not yet," she said. "I'm marrying him."

Grady's eyebrows lifted slightly. "Your man's late," he observed.

"Yes," she said.

She was not annoyed; she was not nervous. She was not afraid of him, and she was not particularly worried because her fiancé had not arrived to meet her. This was a woman who had patience, and who had complete control of herself at all times. He had the peculiar feeling, glancing over at her, that if he were to step over to that chair and bend down and kiss her, she would permit him to do it, and that there would be nothing to it. He would kiss her, and that would be the end of it. She would not scream; she would not resist. She might even smile, and ask him why he'd done it. It would mean nothing to her either way.

He watched the lone rider coming on, and he could make out the color of the horse. It was a black with two white feet. Grady watched and then stepped inside the shack. When he came out he had his gunbelt strapped on.

Lorna Greene said to him, "Why did you do that?"

Grady shrugged. "Who knows?" he said. "This is new country to me, too." He had many questions to ask this woman, because he was curious about her. He did not have any right to ask them, but he was sure she would not particularly mind where another woman would.

"You meet Joe Waddell back east?" he asked.

She looked straight at him, and she smiled again, and when she smiled she was quite pretty. Her teeth were good, and some of the hardness went out of her eyes when she smiled.

"I've never met him," she said. He could not help staring at her. Her smile broadened, and she said, "We have met by correspondence."

Grady Mulvane knew how it was, then, and his estimation of the woman fell accordingly. He'd heard of these correspondence marriages in the West. Lonely men, living out on the ranges, and with no possibility of meeting any kind of women but the bad ones in some of the towns, struck up correspondence with women through the mails. It usually began with an advertisement either the woman or the man put in a magazine or newspaper. It was a case of marrying someone, sight unseen, and the man or woman who did it were usually people who had despaired of any other means of meeting and marrying. It was marriage, but it was not marriage based upon mutual respect and love; it was simply marriage for the sake of marriage.

"You do not approve of such marriages." Lorna Greene smiled.

"No," Grady said.

She wanted an honest answer, and he'd given it to her without hedging.

"I am sorry for that," she said.

Grady was watching the man coming up on the black. He didn't think this man was Joe Waddell. A prospective husband coming to get his bride would not come on a horse to pick up a woman who would be waiting for him at a stage station. Waddell, if he were a nester, would have a buckboard, no matter how ramshackle, and he would come out on it to pick up his woman and her baggage.

"You believe that people should marry in the formal way," Lorna Greene was saying.

"Reckon that's proper," Grady told her.

"Are those marriages always happy ones?" she asked, smiling.

He looked at her and frowned, conscious of the fact that she was chiding him. "Hell of a way to get married," he said. "Marrying a man you've never seen."

"He could prove to be a better husband than a man I've known all my life."

Grady didn't want to argue the point with her. He moved down toward the corral to fetch some water for the horses, and when he came up from the creek with the two pails and dumped the water into the trough, the rider on the black came into the yard.

He was a youngish man, not more than twenty-one or twenty-two, lean, thin-faced, with a narrow chin and blond hair. Grady had his look at him, and didn't like him. He didn't like the shifty, amber-colored eyes. He didn't like the way the blond man looked at Lorne Greene, sitting in her chair under the cottonwood.

"Water my horse?" he said to Grady.

Grady nodded toward the trough. "Drinking water behind the house," he said.

The blond man wasn't even looking at him. He looked at Lorna Greene speculatively, and then he ran his tongue across his thin lips. They were about fifteen yards from where she was sitting, and she couldn't hear them.

"You got a visitor," the blond man grinned.

Grady looked at him. "Waiting for someone to pick her up," he said. "Man named Waddell."

The name seemed to make no impression on the blond man. "Nice for you," he said, "havin' her wait here. She get off that westbound?"

Grady didn't like the remark. "You want to water that horse?" he asked, "or are you here for trouble?"

The blond man wore a big Navy Colt on his right hip, and he seemed very conscious of the gun, and Grady gathered the opinion that he fancied himself more or less of a badman with it. He was grinning now, largely because of the gun, and because he considered himself very dangerous with it.

"Don't talk so big, mister," he warned.

Grady just looked at him, and then he turned and went down to the creek for more water for the teams which had just come in. When he came back he noticed that the blond man's horse was at the trough, but the blond man was back at the shack, talking with Lorna Greene.

She still sat in the chair, looking straight ahead of her, and now there was a slight frown on her face, and Grady Mulvane realized that he would have trouble. He didn't want it with guns because this man was young, and there was no real provocation for the use of guns. The young man would have it that way, though, if he could. Grady had seen enough of them out in this territory to know that.

He walked toward the shack slowly, noticing that the blond man was smoking a cigarette. He'd evidently been saying things and pushing himself, and in a much more ungentlemanly manner than had the passengers on the stage. A young man like this, with a killing or two under his belt, would be like that. He'd walk the earth like a young lion — until a grown lion detoothed him.

Grady said, "Everything all right here, ma'am?"

"Go water your horses, mister," the blond man said contemptuously. To him Grady was just a stock tender, not much of a man or he would not be out here.

Grady looked at him for a moment, and then ignored him as he turned to Lorna Greene again. He said, "He say anything out of the way, Miss Greene?"

The plain affront brought the red to the blond man's face, and he moved away from the wall of the shack where he'd been standing, coming up closer to Grady. "Talk to me," he snapped.

"To hell with you," Grady said.

The blond man's right hand went automatically toward the butt of the big gun protruding from the holster, but Grady was too fast for him.

There was not the savagery in Grady now which had been present when he'd flung himself on top of the fast-moving Ute, nor when he'd gone after the hapless

55

Ed Grubaker, but he moved fast, and there was no mercy in him.

Grasping the younger man's wrist, he held it tightly, preventing him from drawing the gun, and at the same time he came up hard with his shoulder, catching the blond man under the chin with the hard bone and knocking his head up. When he felt the strength go out of his man temporarily, he jerked the hand away from the holster, lifted the gun and tossed it up on the flat roof of the shack. Then he stepped back and swung his right hand in a wide, sweeping movement, the palm open.

The man tried to protect his face with his hand, but Grady's hand got by him, and the slap was audible at the far end of the stone corral. Grady hit his man twice more with the open hand, slashing his guard away, seeing the tears of rage and frustration come to the man's face, and once he cried out from the pain and from the shame of it.

"Please!" Lorna Greene said. "Please, no more."

"Get on your horse," Grady told the blond man. "You can pick up your gun from Ben Champion in Bottle Springs."

The blond man stumbled away, cursing his rage. He jerked his black away from the water trough, pushed up in the saddle, and then rode away hard, never looking behind him. He'd said nothing since Grady started to slap at him, but in his amber eyes was a terrible hatred.

Lorna Greene said, "You've made an enemy."

"Made them before," Grady observed.

56

"This one will try to kill you," she told him. "You didn't have to do that for me."

"I run this station," Grady stated. "He got out of line."

"I am obliged to you again," she said.

Grady shrugged. He put a ladder against the wall of the shack, and then climbed up to retrieve the gun, which he tossed on one of the cots inside. He said when he came out, "You figure your man's coming today?"

"This is the day," Lorna nodded. "We made sure about the details."

"And the place?"

"This is the place."

Grady frowned. It was getting to be late in the afternoon now, and he wondered what he would do if Joe Waddell never arrived.

"I'll go back to Bottle Springs," Lorna Greene said, as if reading his mind, "if Mr. Waddell has changed his mind."

"Just like that?"

"What would you do?" she smiled.

"Shoot him," Grady snapped, "for bringing me way out here. Did he pay your fare?"

"He sent me the fare," Lorna nodded. "One way."

A rider came down the grade from Dutchman's Ridge, and Grady recognized him as Tom O'Hara. The old man hadn't found the runaway horse, but he might be able to help in the matter of finding Joe Waddell, the prospective bridegroom.

When O'Hara dismounted he stared at the girl on the chair, snorted, and then looked at Grady, the question in his blue eyes.

"Came in on the westbound," Grady explained. "Supposed to meet the man she's marrying here."

Tom O' Hara looked at him. "Here?" he asked.

"That's what she says," Grady told him.

"Who's the poor cuss?" the old man asked him, and Grady had to grin a little.

"Joe Waddell," he said.

He saw Tom O'Hara's eyes flick, and then he started to walk slowly toward the girl sitting on the chair.

"She ain't marryin' Joe Waddell," O'Hara said over his shoulder.

Grady walked after him curiously, a little surprised at the old man's remark.

O'Hara pulled up in front of the girl on the chair, and then took off his hat, and this was unusual, too, because Grady had already gathered that the old man had no use for the opposite sex.

"You waitin' here for Joe Waddell?" O'Hara asked.

"Yes," Lorna Greene said.

"To marry him?"

The girl nodded again, and then she glanced at Grady, and for a moment she seemed to lose that air of relaxed composure, and it was another moment before Grady got the point. She thought O'Hara was Joe Waddell!

"Tom O'Hara," Grady said, nodding at the old man. "Works here with me."

58

"Reckon you ain't marryin' Joe Waddell," O'Hara muttered. "Man died last week. Kicked by a damn mule."

Lorna Greene's hands unclasped from her lap, and then she got up from the chair where she'd been sitting and walked slowly to the far end of the shack, and stood there.

Grady said uncomfortably, "Reckon you were traveling, Miss Greene, when he passed away. Wasn't anybody could write to you."

She nodded, and when she turned to face him she was as composed as when she'd gotten off the stage less than thirty minutes ago. She said, "Is there an eastbound stage which will take me back to Bottle Springs this afternoon?"

"Not till the morning," Grady said. He frowned when he looked about, knowing that she couldn't very well stay here. "I'll see if I can get you back to town," he said. "There's a hotel in Bottle Springs."

"I would be obliged to you," she told him.

Grady walked down to the corral where O'Hara was standing, trying to light up a stub of cigar.

"Can we borrow a buckboard around here somewhere?" he asked. "I'll run her into town."

"Fred Anders has a buckboard," O'Hara said. "Lives up the Creek a ways. I'll go git it. Fred's a nester."

Grady said to him, "What about Joe Waddell?"

O'Hara looked at him. "Another nester. Wasn't much this way or that. Just another dirt farmer." He looked back at the girl by the shack and he said, "Reckon Joe was gettin' all the best of this. How in hell he ever met her I'll never know."

"He didn't meet her," Grady explained. "They met by mail."

O'Hara grimaced. "He'd of worked her to the bone. She's got looks now; she wouldn't of had 'em in five years. Why in hell she want to marry him?"

"Ask her," Grady said.

Tom O'Hara didn't ask her. He rode off for the buckboard, and Grady went back to the house.

If the news of her fiancé's death had disturbed her, it no longer showed in her face. She said, "I am sorry to be causing you this much trouble."

"No trouble," Grady assured her. "O'Hara's getting a buckboard. I'll run you in when he gets here."

Lorna Greene looked at him steadily. "What about Mr. Waddell? You were talking about him."

Grady moistened his lips. "You want it straight?" he asked.

"As straight as it is." She half-smiled.

"You're not losing much," Grady assured her. "He was a dirt farmer. He'd have worked you to death."

"Then maybe it's better," Lorna said thoughtfully.

"You'll go back home?"

"I have no home," she told him.

He didn't ask any more questions. It was not his business, and he'd asked a lot of questions already. He found himself relieved, though, that she wasn't marrying Joe Waddell, sight unseen. He didn't know why this should be because he'd met a girl only yesterday who had affected him, emotionally, at least

60

ten times as much as Lorna Greene had, but he was still glad she hadn't been able to go through with a marriage such as this. He told himself that it was because he was sorry for her, but he wasn't exactly sure.

CHAPTER
SIX

It was dusk when Grady Mulvane rode into Bottle Springs, with Lorna. Greene beside him on the buckboard seat and her two bags in the rear. He'd learned a lot more about her on the ride in from Elder Creek. As he'd suspected, she'd been married before, and her husband had died five years ago. She'd been on her own ever since, and she'd lived in a number of places, and not all of them had been pleasant.

She'd never known her mother or father, and she'd been raised by an aunt who had no particular use for her. The aunt was still alive somewhere, but Lorna had no intention of looking her up.

"I'll get by," she'd told Grady.

"What about money?" Grady wanted to know. "You have enough to get back east?"

"Must I go back east?" Lorna smiled.

"There's not much around here," Grady observed. "Not for a woman."

"I'll see," Lorna had told him, and they'd let it rest there.

Grady carried her bags into the lobby of the Bottle Springs Hotel. She again thanked him for his trouble, and they shook hands a little awkwardly, and he went out.

Ben Champion had been lounging out in front of his office, and he was waiting as Grady came out of the hotel.

"I owe you a drink," Grady said.

"Good a time as any," the sheriff said, and they headed for the Cheyenne Bar. "Found yourself some company," he said as they walked down the street.

Grady told him briefly of Lorna Greene's arrival, and then of the necessity of bringing her back to Bottle Springs. Champion listened, saying nothing until Grady had finished, and then he said one word. "Tough."

"Like you to pick up a Navy Colt in the back of the buckboard when we come out," Grady went on. "I took it away from a nasty-mouthed, blond-haired chap."

He gave Ben Champion a description of the blond man, and the sheriff said soberly, "Lee Caspar. You say you slapped his face?"

"Either that," Grady explained, "or shoot him. He was going for his gun."

"He'll try to kill you for that," Champion scowled. "Caspar's a bad one."

"What does he do?" Grady asked.

"He's loose," Ben Champion murmured. "Maybe he likes Well Fargo express boxes. I wouldn't know. You'll have to watch him."

"Figured I would," Grady nodded. "I told him you'd have his gun when he wanted it."

They had their drink at the bar, Grady paying for it with what he had left in his pockets, and then he said, "Your Wells Fargo man came through, I see."

"You saw him, too," Champion smiled. "Not many people missed him, Grady."

"Been any trouble lately?"

"We have a telegraph," Champion told him, "that they hit a Lamonte stage last night a hundred or so miles west of Bottle Springs. They got the express box."

Grady put his glass down on the bar and rubbed his jaw. "That could be the stage I was on," he said. "Man by the name of Buck Neil rode messenger. He'd been drinking." Ben Champion didn't say anything to that, and Grady added, "Lamonte know about his men, or is he easy?"

"He's easy," the sheriff growled. "Tried to talk to him. I've told him he has to tighten things up or he'll be going out of business."

"And it's still no good," Grady said.

"He's in the wrong business," Ben Champion told him, "and the way it's going he won't be in it long."

"Who's his line superintendent?"

"He handles that himself," Champion said.

"Takes a good man to run a stage line," Grady murmured. "Reckon it can get out of hand pretty easy."

He was ready to go, but he still had one request to make of the sheriff.

"The woman I brought in," he said. "She'll be staying at the hotel, I don't know for how long. You could keep an eye on her. She won't know anybody in this town, and I don't know how much money she has — if any."

"Do what I can," Champion nodded. "She headed back east?"

"She wouldn't say," Grady growled. "Seems to have a mind of her own."

"Would you have her any other way?" Champion smiled.

Grady looked at him. "Didn't say I was having her any way," he pointed out.

They went outside and Grady got the gun from the buckboard, handing it to Ben Champion. "This Caspar's in town?" he asked.

"Seen him around," the sheriff nodded. "I didn't know he'd had that trouble with you. I'd walk easy, and I'd have eyes in the back of my head if I were you."

"Aim to," Grady said.

He got into the buckboard and drove it down to the Lamonte Line office, and then he got out and went inside. Jim Lamonte was in the outer office talking to his ticket agent, and he glanced at Grady in surprise when he came in.

"Anything wrong?" he asked.

"Figured I'd tell you why I was in town," Grady smiled. "Somebody might give you a different story tomorrow."

He told Lamonte briefly of the meeting with Lorna Greene, and of the necessity of bringing her back into town tonight.

Jim Lamonte nodded when he'd finished. "You did right," he said. "Is the woman taken care of now?"

"Reckon she'll be all right," Grady told him. "I'm heading out to Elder Springs."

"Anything you need out there?" Lamonte asked him as he bit off the tip of a cigar and put it in his mouth.

"Pretty well fixed," Grady said. He watched Lamonte for a moment, and then he said, "Hear we were hit again."

Lamonte frowned. "Other side of Watch Springs," he said.

Grady looked down at the floor. They'd moved away from the cage where the ticket agent was working, and they were alone for the moment. He said, "You know your shotgun messenger on that trip had been drinking? A man's not liable to take any action, or even shoot straight, if he has liquor in him."

Lamonte shook his head in disgust. "Buck Neil," he said. "I know the man has a drink now and then. I've talked to him about it." He'd been looking at the floor and he looked up at Grady now and smiled. "I dare say, though, you have a drink yourself when you're in town, Mulvane."

"I'm not riding up on that box," Grady pointed out, "with a shotgun across my lap. It makes a difference."

Lamonte nodded. "I'll talk to Neil," he said again, "but it is difficult. We served through the war together. Grubaker was in the same regiment with us. He was a troublemaker, then, too, but he fought under me, and he fought well against the Rebs. It makes it difficult."

Grady looked at the slender man curiously. This was news to him, and it did put a different slant on the

66

matter. Like all old army men, Lamonte was being loyal to the men who'd fought it out with him.

Grady let the matter drop there. Outside on the street he saw Judith Lamonte coming up with another pot of hot coffee for her brother; evidently this was a ritual for them each evening when the brother remained at the office.

"Saw you riding in earlier," Judith said. "Anything go wrong at the station?"

"Had to bring a passenger back," Grady explained, and for the third time he explained about Lorna Greene.

Judith listened carefully, the pain showing in her sensitive eyes when he told her that they'd learned Joe Waddell, the nester, was dead.

"She's alone in town?" Judith said when he'd finished. "I think I'll pay her a visit. She may need help."

Grady was confident of the fact that Lorna Greene could take care of herself, but he said, "She might appreciate that."

When he rode off in the buckboard he was thinking again that Judith Lamonte was a warm-hearted girl, and that Ben Champion was the luckiest man in the West. He considered himself one of the unluckiest for having arrived so late.

It was eight o'clock in the evening when he left Bottle Springs, taking the stage road west toward Elder Creek. He found himself wondering, idly, as he drove along, what Lorna Greene would do. He didn't think she had very much money. A woman with even a little money would never marry a man by chance, especially a woman with some good looks, and he had to concede that Lorna Greene was not too hard to look at.

In the year 1868 it was a difficult matter for a lone woman to make a living. A man could move about; he could work almost anywhere, and do almost any kind of labor. A woman was limited in what she could do, and where she could go.

He'd put two of the chestnuts from the Lamonte corral in the traces of this buckboard, and the animals moved along easily, taking their time. The buckboard Tom O'Hara had borrowed was old, and it squeaked outrageously.

A cool breeze had sprung up as he left town, and there was again a hint of rain in the air. Stars were still sprinkled across the sky, but many of them were being blotted out by fast-moving clouds.

Grady Mulvane relaxed on the seat of the buckboard, and he thought of Judith Lamonte, and then of Lorna Greene, and he wondered about Jim Lamonte, who was headed for bankruptcy unless his line picked up and he was able to stop the holdups. He wondered what Judith would do in a situation like that. Lorna Greene could take care of herself in one way or another; it was a different matter with Judith.

The first drop of rain fell on Grady's face, and it was then that he heard the horseman coming on behind him. He had exceptionally good hearing, partly because he'd lived a good part of his life in the open, and a number of years in the back country where a man's life could depend upon how well he heard things, and partly because he'd been born with the faculty.

He could hear this horseman coming up behind him, but not coming fast. He could hear him even over the racket of the buckboard, and after a while he started to wonder why the rider didn't come up and pass him. The chestnuts were moving at such a slow pace that even jogging along easily, a lone rider would have to pass them, unless he were deliberately remaining behind.

Grady listened carefully, and then he slipped the gun from the holster at his side and placed it on the seat next to him. Ben Champion had warned him to be careful of Lee Caspar, and the chances were that Caspar had either seen him come into town, or watched him leave it.

Grady grimaced, wondering if tonight he would find it necessary to kill a man. If Lee Caspar were trailing him here on this lonely road with the intention of suddenly galloping in and spraying him with lead, the young man deserved to die. But Grady hoped it wouldn't come to that. Caspar would die sooner or later, because his kind did not last too long out in this country, but he wasn't anxious to be instrumental in his death.

He drove on for several more minutes, listening carefully for the horseman behind him, but the man kept his distance. When they came to a small ford over a stream known as Indian Run, Grady stopped to let the horses drink, and when he stopped, the rider behind him stopped too.

There was no doubt in his mind now that a rider was trailing him. What the rider intended to do, Grady still had to find out, but he didn't intend to find out the hard way.

While the horses were drinking, he quickly cut a bunch of branches from the willows along the bank, and he stuffed the leaves into his coat after taking it off and buttoning it. With a piece of rope he found on the floor of the buckboard, he bound the dummy figure to the seat, and then placed his hat upon a few of the branches which protruded up from the collar. He had a reasonable facsimile of a man seated on the box of a buckboard. On a dark night, and with a light rain beginning to fall, it would be quite difficult to ascertain that a switch had been made.

Climbing up to the seat after he had his dummy arranged, Grady pushed the horses across the fording spot and started down the road on the other side. He was about halfway out to Elder Creek, and there was still plenty of time for his pursuer to take action.

Fifty yards down the stage road, Grady slipped from the seat, sliding to the rear of the buckboard. He lay on his back, then, gun in hand, and he let the horses pick their own easy way down the road.

He lay there, the light, cooling rain falling on his face, his body completely relaxed, taking the bumps in the road, wondering why it was that men like Lee Caspar had to rub people the wrong way, and sometimes die for it.

There was still the possibility that the man behind him was not Caspar, but Ed Grubaker, who also hated

70

him, and might like to put a bullet in his back. Grady considered the two men, and came to the conclusion that it was more likely to be Caspar.

For fully ten minutes Grady lay on the floor of the buckboard, and then his man made his play. He heard the horse coming on quickly, and he tightened his grip on the gun in his hand, still remaining flat on his back.

The rider was on top of the buckboard very suddenly, coming up on the right side. A gun banged rapidly three times in succession, and then the rider swerved off the road.

Grady came up on his knees, and he managed to get one shot off at the disappearing rider, but he didn't think he'd hit the man. The quick shots had sent the horses running, and the buckboard was bouncing badly as he tried to take aim.

The dummy figure on the front seat fell back into the rear of the buckboard as Grady grabbed up the reins and in a few moments managed to bring the horses to a halt.

He listened carefully, and he could hear a horse running in the distance, moving farther and farther away. Whether it had been Lee Caspar or Ed Grubaker he didn't know.

When he took the coat from the dummy figure he'd made of the branches, he felt with his finger and discovered two holes in the back of the coat. Had he been sitting up on that seat, he'd be dead.

Feeling the holes with his finger, Grady Mulvane was sure of one thing. He owed a man something for this attack in the dark, and he intended to pay it.

CHAPTER
SEVEN

Ed Grubaker came through the next morning on the box of the westbound, and he was sullen and silent as he remained up on the seat while Grady and Tom O'Hara changed the horses. A man whom Grady did not know sat beside him, riding messenger. Grubaker's face was still bruised from the battering Grady had given him, and one eye was discolored, but he was able to handle his teams. He sat on the box, staring straight ahead of him, and had nothing to say.

Once when Grady was coming by with the swing team, he paused and said quietly, "Doing any night riding recently, Grubaker?"

Grubaker stared down at him, the perplexity coming into his eyes. "What the hell does that mean?" he asked, and Grady knew that it hadn't been Grubaker. The driver had been honestly puzzled by the question.

"You don't figure it was Grubaker?" Tom O'Hara asked as the stage rolled away.

"It wasn't Grubaker," Grady said. "That leaves Caspar."

"He'll try it again," O'Hara observed. "That kind always does."

"The next time he won't ride off," Grady murmured.

The morning stage hadn't provided any excitement, but the afternoon eastbound did. The driver, a man by the name of Hendricks, jumped down from the box immediately after slipping his brake handle into the notch. He looked a little pale around the gills, and he jerked his head toward the roof of the stage as he came down, saying to Grady, "Take a look."

Grady went up on the roof, and the first thing he saw as his head came over the top of the guard rail was a man's boot, and then another. A body lay wrapped in a tarpaulin on the roof.

Frowning, Grady moved up toward the head and pulled back the tarpaulin. The dead man was the Wells Fargo agent who'd ridden by the day before. He'd been shot through the back of the head, and the lead had come out just above his right eyebrow. There was not much blood, just the ugly, purplish hole.

Grady climbed down from the roof after replacing the tarpaulin. He said to the driver, "Where did it happen?"

"Found him half a dozen miles up along the creek, layin' right off the stage road. Figured it was a drunk when I first saw him. Dead as hell, though."

Tom O'Hara had climbed up to have a look, also, and he came down, his face grim.

"Bushwhacker," he said.

"Couldn't let him lay there," the driver muttered. "Figured we'd bring him in to Bottle Springs. Anybody know him?"

"We ain't sure," O'Hara scowled. "Ask Ben Champion; ask Lamonte."

When the stage had gone on, the old man said, "Wells Fargo man. Means they're throwin' lead now."

"Who?" Grady asked him.

"You tell me," O'Hara muttered. "Figured that one wouldn't last long, though."

"They'll send out another man," Grady observed. "Maybe two."

"Won't stop 'em if they don't want to be stopped," O'Hara said. "This crowd is organized. It knows what in hell it's doin'."

Grady sat down on the bench out in front of the shack and watched the stage rolling east up toward Dutchman's Ridge.

"Who's the smartest man in Bottle Springs?" he asked.

Tom O'Hara said promptly, "Lace Madison. Runs the Diamond Stud. Only establishment in town has women workin' the customers for the percentage on drinks."

Grady had noticed the place, but hadn't been inside it the few times he'd been in Bottle Springs. The Diamond Stud was a combination saloon and gambling hall, and without money in his pockets, Grady had stayed away from a house like that.

"If Madison does well with the Diamond Stud," Grady observed, "why would he be interested in the Wells Fargo boxes?"

"Man can always do better," O'Hara said sagely, "an' he can do it a lot quicker workin' the Lamonte stages."

"Is he honest?" Grady asked.

74

Tom O'Hara grinned. "Who's honest, when fifty thousand in currency is goin' by in a iron box strapped to the floor of a stage."

Grady considered this fact. With the Wells Fargo man out of the way, and possibly some delay before they could get another detective out this way, it meant that if Jim Lamonte had to be helped, somebody else had to do the helping. Helping Jim Lamonte, of course, meant helping Judith, also, and Grady Mulvane was not unaware of this fact.

He wished now that he were able to spend a little more time in town to look around, to listen to the talk, and possibly to do a little riding, but this was out of the question unless he took things in his own hands.

His mind was made up for him that evening, though, when Ben Champion rode out to Elder Creek on his way through to Sherman City.

"Have to make a check in Sherman City about that Wells Fargo man," the sheriff scowled. "I don't figure I'll be able to learn anything, but it has to be done."

"Nothing in Bottle Springs?" Grady asked him.

"What can you learn in Bottle Springs?" Champion said gruffly. "Nobody will talk, either, now that a man's been killed."

"Nearly had another killed last night," Grady observed, and he told Champion about the attack made on him in the buckboard.

"You think it was Lee Caspar?"

Grady nodded.

"He'll try again," the sheriff said.

"The next time he won't ride away from it," Grady promised.

The sheriff of Bottle Springs had some further information. "That woman you brought in last night," Champion said. "Goes by the name or Lorna Greene?"

"She pull out?" Grady asked him.

"Reckon she's stayin'," Champion told him. "Took a job at Lace Madison's."

Grady stared at him. "Diamond Stud?" he asked.

"Percentage girl," Champion nodded. "Seems like she's able to take care of herself, though."

Grady was fairly sure of that. He remembered that Lorna Greene had a peculiar detached way about her which would enable her to take care of herself as far as men were concerned, but he didn't like the thought of her working in a gambling establishment.

"Reckon her money was gone," Champion said. "She got a rough deal there with Joe Waddell dying, but then she may have gotten a worse if he'd lived. *Quien sabe.*"

When the sheriff rode off, Grady sat down on the bench in front of the shack and stared into the gathering dusk. He rolled a cigarette, smoked it halfway through, and then tossed it away, and he got up and walked down to the corral.

The night was clear after the brief rain the previous evening, and the smell of sage was heavy in the air. The horses which had come in on the late afternoon westbound were still in the corral, dark shapes against the night sky.

76

Tom O'Hara passed by and said casually, "That black up in the shed ain't been up on its feed for a long time. Been thinkin' of takin' her up to Doc Watson's. He works on horses as well as humans."

Grady waited, knowing what the older man was coming around to.

"Reckon you might just as well take her in as me," O'Hara said, "an' tonight's as good a night as any other. Nothin' due here till the westbound comes through in the mornin'."

"I could ride in," Grady murmured.

O'Hara had one more thing to say. "I don't figure you're gettin' her to quit that job, though."

Grady smiled. "Maybe not," he said.

"What's a woman supposed to do when she's broke?" O'Hara asked.

"There must be other work in town."

"Like what?" O'Hara persisted. "Who knows her? Who trusts her?"

Grady said no more on the subject. He saddled the gray gelding and put a halter on the ailing black, and he rode off into the night, taking the stage road east to Bottle Springs. He had his legitimate reason for going into town, but Tom O'Hara had provided it for him.

He was curious, too, to meet Lace Madison. Tom O'Hara had a good head, and living out here on the edge of nothing, he did a great deal of straight thinking, and he was thinking that Madison might know something about the raids on the Lamonte stages. Tom O'Hara was not the kind of man, either, who went only on hunches . . .

Grady left Elder Creek and rode in to Bottle Springs at about nine o'clock in the evening. He left the black at Doc Watson's, reported to the station agent that he'd left a horse in town, and walked toward the Diamond Stud.

He wondered if he'd find Lee Caspar in town, and if he did, what would come out of it. He knew that this time when he left Bottle Springs he'd be on his guard, and he'd be riding a fast horse. His man would never ride away from another ambush.

Lace Madison's establishment occupied an entire corner, a two-story frame building with a huge porch. The Diamond Stud drew most of the well-heeled crowd in and around Bottle Springs, but Grady was a little surprised, when he pushed in through the doors, to meet Jim Lamonte at a nearby card table.

The owner of Lamonte Line looked at him curiously, and Grady realized that he owed the man an explanation for coming into town on two successive nights.

There were two other men in the card game with Lamonte, and he had a drink at his elbow when Grady came up. There had been no avoiding the man even if Grady had wished to do so. Lamonte's head had turned toward him when he came into the gambling house.

Grady said, "Had to bring one of the animals in. O'Hara thinks it's down with the colic."

Lamonte nodded. "Have a drink. Tell the bartender it's on me."

"I'm obliged," Grady said.

He moved off, walking between the tables toward the bar, looking over the women who were in the place. He counted four of them, but he didn't see Lorna Greene immediately. They were all flashily dressed, and a red-haired girl came toward him as he approached the bar, but Grady shook his head at her, and she turned away.

Apparently the main games were upstairs. He thought he could hear the whir of a roulette wheel, and a keno man calling his numbers.

A bartender came over toward him, wiping the bar with a rag, and he grinned and said, "Rough man from Lamonte Line."

"Lamonte's buying me a drink," Grady said, and he pointed to a bottle on the shelf behind the bartender. He hadn't asked or expected Jim Lamonte to buy him a drink, but it would have been an affront refusing it. Lamonte was a square shooter; he treated his employees as equals.

"Hear they shot up a man out your way," the bartender said as he got the bottle and a glass.

Grady nodded, giving him no more information. He looked about the room, wondering if Lorna Greene were upstairs, wondering what he would say to her when she came down. He was wondering, too why he'd even come in here, but he felt that he had to talk to her. If she had one friend in this town, he was it. He'd been involved in a fight because of her, and he made an enemy who'd tried to kill him. For this reason, if for no other, he had the right to talk to her.

He lingered over his drink, wondering if he'd have to go upstairs, and then he saw her coming down. She had her hair done up differently, and at first he did not recognize her. She wore a pink dress with flashing sequins, and the dress was cut low. She had a full, rich figure, and the men at the tables turned to watch her as she came down.

She didn't walk like the other women in the Diamond Stud. She had her head up high, and the smile on her face was genuine. When she saw him at the bar, she nodded pleasantly, but at the bottom of the stairs a man spoke to her, and she cleverly disengaged his arm, gave him a smile, and moved toward the bar. O'Hara had been right, and so had Ben Champion; she could take care of herself, here or anywhere.

She said when she came up, "I see I don't have to persuade you to buy drinks, Grady."

"Not me," Grady growled.

"How are you?" she asked.

"How are you?" he snapped, "and what in hell are you doing in a place like this?"

"It's a job," she said, and the surprise showed in her mild brown eyes at the anger in his voice.

"You shouldn't be here," he grated. "It's not a job for a lady."

A lanky man, half drunk, came by and took her by the arm. Grady slapped his hand away, and the drunk turned on him as if wanting to make something of it.

The bartender said casually, "Back off, George. That's the hombre damn near killed Ed Grubaker the other night."

80

George did back off, grumbling to himself as he did so, and Grady said sourly to Lorna, "What would you have done if I weren't here?"

"Have him buy a few drinks," Lorna smiled. "That's my job."

"I might be able to borrow twenty-five dollars," Grady said. "You can have it to get the next stage east."

"I'm not going," Lorna said evenly. "I'm obliged to you for the offer." She was watching him coolly as she stood at the bar, and she added, "Why do you want me out of this town?"

"Out of this place," Grady snapped. "You can stay in the town if you wish."

"Not without money. This is the only place I could get work."

A man was, coming down along the bar, a big man with solid shoulders and blond hair which caught the gleam of the hanging lamps along the bar. He was smiling, and his teeth were white and even, a rarity in these Western states. His clothes were neat and clean, too — expensive, fawn-colored pants and a brown jacket. His boots were of brown leather, richly tooled. In dress he could be considered almost a dude, but the solid jaw, and the glint in his blue-gray eyes made Grady look at him twice. This was not a man to take lightly.

"New customer?" the tall man smiled.

Grady looked at him, This, then, was Lace Madison, owner of the Diamond Stud.

"Grady Mulvane," Lorna introduced them. "Lace Madison, my employer."

"You've got the wrong girl here," Grady said. "Trying to convince her to leave."

Madison lifted his eyebrows slightly. "You're the man had the fight with Grubaker," he murmured. "Heard of you. Why do you want Miss Greene to leave?"

"Not the kind of job for her," Grady told him.

Madison shrugged. "You offering her a better one?" he smiled.

"I'm not making any offers," Grady told him.

Lace Madison patted him gently on the shoulder before moving on to Jim Lamonte's table. He said softly, "Maybe, then, you'd better let her alone, Mr. Mulvane. We like her here."

Grady stared after his broad back, watched him nod in friendly fashion to Lamonte and the other men, and then sit down in the game. Apparently he was on good terms with the owner of Lamonte Line.

Madison had given him a little warning, too, to stay out of things which did not concern him, and a warning from Lace Madison, Grady realized instinctively, was not something you could shrug off.

Lorna said, "I'm sorry if I've displeased you, Grady. Do stop in again. I'll always be glad to see you."

"We'll see," Grady growled, and he nodded to her and started for the door.

Jim Lamonte didn't see him go out, but Lace Madison did, and he glanced up and smiled at Grady as he passed. There was neither warmth nor unfriendliness in the smile. Lace Madison just smiled, and a man could make what he wanted out of it.

Pushing out through the batwing doors, Grady paused for a moment on the porch. He was standing in the full light of the inside lamps, and even before the gun sounded from across the road he realized that this was a mistake which could easily have cost him his life, considering what had happened the previous night on the way back to Elder Creek.

CHAPTER
EIGHT

The gun had the heavy boom of a big Navy Colt, and Lee Caspar had been wearing a Navy Colt when Grady had taken it away from him. Grady saw the flash of orange-red light from a doorway almost directly opposite the Diamond Stud. The lead whacked into one of the porch pillars inches to his left, and waist high.

Without even pulling his own gun, Grady fell to the floor, rolling toward the right. The man across the road fired again, and then a third time, but the porch was several feet high, and Grady, lying flat now and out of the light, was a bad target.

He kept rolling toward the far end of the porch, and then he rolled completely off the porch, his body striking the soft earth out of range of the killer across the street.

His gun was in his hand now. He lifted his head cautiously above the rim of the porch, saw no movement across the road, and then he sprinted across, waiting for the first flash of the gun.

When it didn't come he knew that his man had run again — but tonight he wouldn't be able to run fast or far enough.

The shots had come from a doorway, and Grady could see now that the killer had been inside an abandoned building, standing just inside the door, and firing from that position.

The building probably had been a saloon. The windows had been boarded up, and the door was loose on its hinges. Instead of going through the building, Grady took the faster way up the alley on the left, confident that his man would emerge at the rear and keep going.

He ran hard, stumbling through the trash in the alley, nearly falling once, and when he reached the far end of the alley he caught a glimpse of a man running off toward his right. He sent one shot after the fleeing figure, and then took off after him.

It was dark here in the vacant lots behind the buildings along the main street, and Grady was on unfamiliar territory. He'd also underestimated the cleverness of the man he was chasing. The first mistake undoubtedly saved his life.

He was running too fast and too hard in the darkness, not knowing what was in front of him, and he ran full into an upended abandoned table which had been thrown out here.

The table leg caught him in the middle, taking the breath out of him as he spun around it, falling heavily to the ground just as a gun banged from a point not ten feet away. He'd been running full into an ambush.

As his body hit the ground he fired, not seeing anything, but throwing lead anyway to disconcert the man in front of him, and then he heard running steps again, and he scrambled to his feet.

He'd scraped the knuckles of his gun hand as he went down on the ground, and he knew that they were raw and bleeding. His stomach hurt where he'd hit the hard end of the table leg, but he kept running, now and then catching glimpses of the man ahead of him.

He realized that there would be no stopping this fight until one of them was dead. Ben Champion, who might have intervened, was on his way out to Sherman City, and any other man in town would have been a fool to try to stop this.

The killer cut down an alley, heading back toward the main street, and Grady drove after him. When he reached the main street again, he saw his man sprinting toward a group of horses tied out in front of one of the saloons. When the man passed a patch of light He recognized him as Lee Caspar. The shifty-eyed blond man had tried to kill him last night, and he'd made another attempt tonight.

Caspar's black with the two white feet was in the group of horses out in front of the saloon, and Caspar vaulted into the saddle as Grady came down the street after him.

Saloons had emptied at the sounds of the shots, and men watched Grady silently as he whipped past them, heading for his own gray, which he'd left in the alley next to the stage depot.

He saw Lace Madison and Jim Lamonte out in front of the Diamond Stud watching him as he went by, and he thought he heard Lamonte call out, but there was no stopping him now. It was not in Lamonte's province to stop him, either, because this was not a Lamonte Line affair.

Grady whirled the gray out of the alley and took the stage road west in the direction of Elder Creek, following less than a hundred yards behind Lee Caspar.

There was no moon tonight, but plenty of starlight, and he could keep his man in sight easily. The gray was the bigger and stronger horse, and it was only a matter of time, Grady knew, before he came up with his man.

He didn't think Caspar would head straight out for Elder Creek, and so he was not surprised when the thin man pulled his black off the road and headed into the hills when they were less than a mile out of town.

Grady took after him, the gray beginning to gain now. He had a hunch that Caspar was heading for a hide-out of some kind where he could fort up and make a fight of it. Caspar lacked the courage to stand up to him and throw lead, but if he were behind a wall he would fight like a cornered rat. Grady was convinced that he was heading for a wall, any kind of wall.

Less Caspar's black went up a slight grade, disappearing over the top, and Grady went after him, gun drawn now, watching for those ambushes which Caspar seemed to love so much.

After they left the stage road they passed groups of cattle standing in dark, huddled bunches. It could mean that there would be a line camp along here somewhere, a camp Lee Caspar would probably know about.

They came upon the hut quite suddenly. Grady was less than fifty yards behind his man when Caspar rode up to a stone hut, threw himself from the saddle, let the black run, and then darted in through the open door of the hut.

Grady left the saddle a moment later, and none too soon. Lee Caspar's gun started to bark from the window as Grady dropped flat on his face and lay there, not moving. The gray ran on along a ridge, and then stopped running, and Grady watched the animal from where he lay.

Lee Caspar had fired several shots, but now he was silent as he waited for Grady to reveal himself. He had all the advantage now, protected behind the stone walls of the hut, but he could not see Grady. A man moving could be seen against the night sky, but a man flat on the ground blended with the shadows.

Grady Mulvane lay there, breathing easily. He'd stalked wild horses, and he had plenty of patience, and tonight it was going to take time. Lee Caspar had seen his horse running on, and he knew his man was out here in the darkness. He would let the pressure rest upon Caspar now. He didn't think Caspar would be able to hold up under it.

For about ten minutes Grady lay quietly, and then very carefully, moving inch by inch, he rolled over and lay on his back, looking up at the night sky.

Caspar yelled from the stone hut, "Come an' get it, Mulvane. I got plenty of lead waitin' for you."

88

Grady smiled and closed his eyes. Knowing his man, he realized that Caspar would be afraid to run, and afraid to come out of his hut after him.

Caspar yelled a few more insults, but when Grady said nothing in return, Caspar finally stopped. He fired a few shots in the direction he thought Grady might be, but he was twenty yards off. Grady had protected himself by lying behind a slight rise in the ground.

Caspar could never know in which direction his man had gone after throwing himself from his horse. He would only know that Grady was still here because the horse was out on the ridge in plain sight. Possibly he could have circled the hut completely and was now crawling in the opposite side, coming right up to the wall of the hut.

When Caspar stopped yelling, Grady went off to sleep. He wasn't sure how long he slept, but he was awakened by Lee Caspar's shooting again, and shouting. From the position of the stars he figured that nearly an hour had gone by.

Lee Caspar was yelling obscene insults at him, and he was shooting his gun far off toward Grady's left now, and then he threw more lead out another window in exactly the opposite direction.

It was still fairly early in the evening, and as the hours passed, each one would take its toll on Lee Caspar. He could not attempt to sleep, because any moment his man might come in through the doorway, or appear at the window. He had to be vigilant every moment, and after a while the pressure would begin to tell.

Casper ran out of insults, and he was quiet again. Grady could picture him inside the hut, cursing to himself, his hand sweaty as it held the gun, watching the window, watching through the doorway, crossing to look out through the other window opening, not sure of anything, listening for a man's breathing close up to the wall of the hut.

If Grady had fired a shot or two at the hut, or called back to him, it would have relieved the pressure, but the silence was killing. They were alone in the night, and it was another seven hours at least till dawn. Lee Caspar would never last seven hours. Grady Mulvane was confident of that. He could not stand two more hours of this silence.

Lee Caspar lasted less than an hour. He'd been in the hut for over two hours, waiting for his man to show himself, or to throw lead, or to speak. He'd heard and seen nothing, and it was too much for him. Grady imagined that he'd wasted more than half his lead shooting at shadows, and now he made his play.

"I'm comin' out, Mulvane," he yelled suddenly, and there was a touch of hysteria in his voice. "You hear me? I'm comin' out."

Grady had placed his Colt gun at his side when he lay down. He reached for it now, spinning the cylinder once, and then he was ready. He was lying on his stomach, facing the stone hut, and he pushed the gun forward, waiting.

Lee Caspar came out of the hut like a wild man, circling it, firing at every shadow against the wall, and then he stopped when he realized Grady was not up against the wall, but still out in the open somewhere.

Even from the distance, Grady could hear his heavy, agonized breathing. He felt a touch of pity for the man, but then he remembered that Lee Caspar had fired at him twice from ambush, and he would do it again if he got away tonight. He was a mad dog who had to be treated as a mad dog, and there was only one treatment for a mad dog. Grady Mulvane waited.

Lee Caspar lurched away from the hut, swinging off at an angle from Grady. He acted like a drunken man, hatless, his gun in his hand, swaying as he walked. Again he fired, and then he had to stop to reload, and Grady could have gotten up and shot him to death right there, but he waited until Caspar had more lead in his gun, and he waited until Caspar eventually came in his direction. He waited until Lee Caspar was not more than ten yards from where he lay, and then he spoke for the first time since this strange siege had begun. He said gently, "This way, Caspar."

Lee Caspar's gun roared. He fired hastily, wildly, and Grady fired once, aiming at Caspar's middle.

The younger man's body broke as the slug took him above the belt. He doubled up, and then he went down on both knees, and he lay that way, and Grady could see his head rocking from side to side, and then quite slowly he lowered his body to the ground.

After a while Grady got up, stiffness in him now, and he walked forward. He could see the starlight glint on

Lee Caspar's gun, still in his outstretched hand, and he kicked the gun away.

Then he rolled the body over, lit a match, had his look, and blew out the match. Lee Caspar would never again shoot at a man from ambush.

It was another half-hour before Grady had mounted his gelding and located Caspar's black. He led the animal back to the hut, tied Caspar's body across the saddle, and then headed back for Bottle Springs.

It was past one o'clock in the morning when he returned, but people had been hearing the distant shooting, off and on, and a lot of them were waiting. The word spread rapidly as he made his appearance at the west end of town, and as he came down the main street, leading the black with Lee Caspar's body tied across the saddle, men came out of the various saloons and stood there watching him silently.

Grady stopped at the first saloon, and he said, "Where's the coroner in this town?"

The man to whom he spoke called over his shoulder, "Fred Branston?"

A man came down the steps to take the reins of the black horse.

"He have anybody?" Grady asked.

"Not that I know of," the coroner said.

"The horse and trappings should pay for it," Grady said.

"It'll pay for it," Fred Branston told him.

A larger crowd was out in front of the Diamond Stud a few paces down the street, and Grady rode on there, seeing Jim Lamonte on the porch. He said succinctly,

"Reckon I'll be riding out to Elder Creek now, Mr. Lamonte."

"You could stand a drink first," Lamonte invited.

Grady tied the gray to the tie-rack, ducked under it, and pushed through the crowd on the porch. They were staring at him curiously.

"Took a long time," one man said.

Grady looked at him. "Was there a hurry?" he asked, and the man said nothing. He'd simply made a comment, and he was even backing away from that now.

Inside, Grady pulled up at the bar with Jim Lamonte, and the respectful bartender brought them a bottle and two glasses.

Lamonte said, "You're as bad with a gun as with your fists, Mulvane."

"He threw the first shot," Grady observed, "and he tried to gun me last night."

"Everybody knows that," Lamonte nodded. "There were men in the street who saw Caspar fire at you from that abandoned saloon."

Lace Madison came up and joined them, that smile still on his face.

"You go for your man, Mulvane," he murmured, "and you get him. Who can ask for more than that?"

Grady looked at him and said nothing. He downed the drink before him, and then he saw Lorna Greene over by the far wall watching him, and his anger rose against Madison again. He said to the gambling hall owner, "I still think you picked the wrong girl for this job, Madison."

Lace shrugged. "You're back on that again," he said. "Why not forget it, unless this girl means something to you."

Grady had nothing to say about that. He was thinking, though, that it would be a hell of a thing if he fell for a percentage girl, and a girl, also, who'd come out to this country to marry a man she'd never seen.

Jim Lamonte said, "Everything all right out at Elder Creek, Mulvane?"

"For me," Grady nodded, "and for O'Hara. Reckon that Wells Fargo man didn't do too well."

Lamonte frowned. "Ben Champion checked his identification. He was a Wells Fargo special agent."

"He didn't last long," Grady observed, "and they're still hitting your stages, Mr. Lamonte."

Jim Lamonte didn't say anything to that, and Grady had the feeling that Lamonte would appreciate it if he kept his mouth shut, too, on this touchy subject.

"Reckon I'll ride out," Grady said, and Lamonte just nodded.

Walking toward the door, Grady saw Lorna Greene angling toward him, and he waited for her to come up. She said when she stopped in front of him, "You're all right? You weren't hurt?"

Grady looked down at her, saw the concern in her brown eyes, and reflected that it was the first time in his life a woman had been concerned about him. It had to be a woman like this, a woman other men pawed; a woman who earned her living in a way decent women despised.

94

Just thinking about it angered him, and he said gruffly, "Reckon I'm all right."

All the way back to Elder Creek he was in a bad mood.

CHAPTER
NINE

Two days later Ben Champion came back from Sherman City on the eastbound, and he was in a bad mood, too. He had his horse tied to the rear boot of the stage, and when the big Concord rolled into the yard he stepped down and untied the horse, intending to ride the rest of the way in to Bottle Springs.

Grady and Tom O'Hara were busy for a few minutes changing the teams, and the sheriff moved back to the shack for a drink of water from the bucket. He was sitting on the bench smoking a cigarette, when the stage rolled on, and Grady went back to join him as O'Hara watered the horses which had just come in.

Grady said to him as he sat down on the bench, "Learn anything?"

"Not a damn thing," Champion growled. "They're clever. They know about everything."

"Then it comes from the inside," Grady observed. "What about that cashier at the stage office in Bottle Springs?"

"Known him for twenty years," Champion said. "He's as honest as the day is long."

"Could be anybody, then," Grady said. "Anybody from here to Sherman City and back."

96

"They hit another stage," Champion said, "between Wind River and Jack's Station."

Grady frowned. "Who was on the box?" he asked.

"Ed Grubaker and Buck Neil."

"Damned if I'd trust either one of them," Grady said, "but Lamonte holds on to them because they're old army mates."

"Jim wouldn't fire men on mere suspicion." Ben Champion grimaced. "And I couldn't arrest them on that." He watched Grady carefully, and said, "Hear you had a little trouble, yourself."

"Lee Caspar tried it again," Grady said. "He didn't make it."

"Sooner or later," Champion said morosely, "his kind always runs into a better man. I can't hold you for anything. All the reports I hear say that Caspar tried to gun you from cover. You were in Lace Madison's to see the girl?"

"I saw her," Grady nodded.

"And you couldn't get her out."

Grady scowled. "Reckon she's old enough to know what the hell she's doing." He looked down at the tips of his boots and he said, "What about Madison?"

"What about him?" Champion smiled.

"I don't like him," Grady said, "and Tom O'Hara figures he could be mixed up in these holdups in one way or another."

"I can't hang a man for that," Champion said gently. "Give me a little more evidence, Grady."

"That's all I have," Grady said. "O'Hara figures he's smart to know where big money is and to go after it when it's to be had. He wouldn't take a gun and get behind a mask, himself, but he could arrange a thing like that."

"He could," Champion nodded, "and so could another hundred and fifty men between here and Sherman City."

Grady could see the logic in that. He said, "Wells Fargo sending another man out?"

"Have to," Champion told him, "or stop shipping over Lamonte Line, and they don't want to do that. Lamonte notified Wells Fargo that their first man hadn't made it."

"Second man won't make it, either," Grady scowled, "unless he's a hell of a lot smarter than the first."

Ben Champion rode off half an hour later, and Grady, with time on his hands now that the last stage for the day had gone through, decided to saddle the gray and have a look for the runaway bay horse which Tom O'Hara had been unable to find.

O'Hara said to him as he was saddling up, "Kind of quiet around here, ain't it, Grady?"

Grady shrugged. "It's a job," he said.

He rode due west, moving along Elder Creek, passing one or two nester shacks. The second one was about five miles up along the. Creek, and it seemed deserted. Riding closer, he noticed that the sheds were empty, and there wasn't any smoke coming from the chimney.

This undoubtedly was the homestead of Joe Waddell, whom Lorna Greene had contracted to marry. It was a mean, slovenly-looking place, and Grady wondered what lies the dead man had told Lorna in order to get her out here. He wondered if she would have stayed after seeing the place and meeting Joe Waddell.

There was a vegetable patch overrun with weeds, and a few scraggly cottonwoods providing meager shade around the house. A half-starved, half-wild mongrel dog came out to bark at him as he rode by, and Grady was tempted to put a bullet through the animal to end its miseries, but the dog ran off.

Looking at the place, he wondered how badly off Lorna Greene had been that she would take the long chance of spending her life in a hovel like this. She had undoubtedly come to the end of her rope, and he felt himself feeling sorry for her, and even condoning to some extent her action in taking the job at the Diamond Stud . . .

Riding on past the Waddell place he entered a country of barren yellow hills which seemed to stretch on endlessly toward the west. There were occasional cattle tracks, but he saw nothing of the bay horse, and after half an hour of riding through the hills, he swung east and north, moving in the general direction of Bottle Springs.

He must have been three or four miles from town when he saw the rider on the chestnut horse moving down a little stream which flowed into Elder Creek. Grady had been heading for the stream to let the gray drink, and he continued his course now even though the rider was coming directly toward him.

When they were less than fifty yards apart he recognized the rider as Judith Lamonte. She was in riding costume, fawn-colored riding pants and a white blouse. Her dark hair was tucked in under a black, flat-crowned hat.

Evidently, she hadn't seen him until their paths started to converge, and then it was a little too late to change her course, even though she might not have been too anxious to meet a strange rider out here in the country. When she recognized Grady, he saw the relief come to her face, and she smiled at him as he touched his hat. In a riding costume, or dressed for town, he was convinced that she was by far the most beautiful girl he'd seen in his life, and the beauty was more than skin deep. She had a warmth to her, and a genuine goodness of heart. He remembered her kindness to him when he'd come in from the mountains looking like a run-down saddletramp.

Both dismounted to water the horses, and Grady said to her, "You ride often, Miss Lamonte?"

"I love it," she told him.

"Been out looking for a horse that broke away from the corral," Grady explained. "No luck yet."

Judith nodded, and then she looked at him thoughtfully. "I heard about your trouble in town the other night," she said.

Grady frowned. "I don't like to kill a man," he said. "This one asked for it." He paused and then said, "I understand things are still going pretty badly with Lamonte Line."

Judith nodded. "They've been unable to stop the holdups," she admitted. "I don't know what Jim's going to do."

"I know what I'd do," Grady told her.

"You'd ride the box, yourself," she smiled, "with a shotgun across your lap, and they wouldn't hold up your stages."

Grady grinned. Changing the subject he said, "You come from the East?"

"Indiana," she told him. "How do you like it at Elder Creek?"

"Damned quiet," Grady said. "I was broke and I needed the pay."

"Possibly Jim can find you other work," she said.

When she said it, it suddenly struck Grady that the kind of job he wanted was probably begging applicants. He'd noticed that on a number of stages Lamonte didn't have shotgun messengers, which probably meant that Lamonte hadn't been able to hire men for this dangerous job. It was the kind of work he would like to do, and he was sure he'd give the road agents a rough time before they took away a Wells Fargo box.

He said, "I might ride into town and talk to your brother about that. Running a swing station is for a man who likes to sit and smoke a pipe."

"You're not that man," Judith smiled. "I'll tell Jim you're coming in."

"Better still," Grady said hesitantly, "I could ride in with you."

"That would be nice," Judith nodded.

He had another question for her as they mounted and turned their horses in the direction of Bottle Springs. He had to know the answer to this one because it would have a bearing on his future conduct. He wanted to get around to the question casually and indirectly, but it was against his nature, and realizing that he would get an honest answer from her, he put it quite bluntly.

He said, "Are you thinking of marrying Ben Champion, Miss Lamonte?"

"I don't know," she confessed after a moment's pause. "I like Ben, and I've known him for several years. I don't really know if I'm going to marry him."

"Reckon that's fair enough," Grady said.

"Why do you ask?"

"I wanted to know," Grady said gravely, and there was no more either of them could say now because a rider was approaching, coming from the direction of Bottle Springs. The horse was a big bay animal, and the rider was Lace Madison. He had been coming in the same direction which Judith Lamonte had taken from Bottle Springs, and Grady was positive it was more than a coincidence.

When he saw the expression on Madison's face as he came up closer, he was convinced of the fact. Madison was smiling and affable as usual, but deep down in his blue-gray eyes there was that slight hint of annoyance that Grady had happened along.

"Out for a ride, Judith?" he asked the girl.

"I met up with Grady down at Little Creek," Judith told him. "We're riding in to see Jim now."

"How nice," Lace Madison murmured. "Things pretty slow at Elder Creek, Mulvane?"

"Moving fast enough," Grady said flatly, knowing what he was driving at. "I'm out looking for a stray horse."

He knew something else about this man now. Ben Champion had another rival for the affections of Judith Lamonte. Grady wondered grimly how many others there were in this part of the country who had fallen for the girl.

They rode on in to Bottle Springs, Grady having little to say now that Lace Madison had joined them. He found himself liking this smooth, affable man less and less as they rode along, and he wondered if it were only because of Judith.

In Bottle Springs, Lace rode on with Judith to the stable where she kept her chestnut, and Grady dismounted out in front of the Lamonte office to see Jim Lamonte.

Lamonte was sitting at his desk when Grady walked in, and he lifted his eyebrows in surprise at seeing him. Very briefly, Grady made his request, confident that Lamonte would be glad to switch him around to shotgun messenger aboard one of his stages. It was difficult enough getting men to accept that dangerous position.

Lamotne heard him through, saying nothing until Grady had finished, and then he stared down at the floor as he rubbed his chin. Then he said slowly, "Mulvane, put yourself in my position. I run a stage line which is being hit by road agents. I don't know who they are. If the trouble continues I'm out of business. You can see that."

103

"I can see it," Grady nodded, wondering what he was coming around to.

"A stranger rides into town, looking, if you'll pardon me, like a saddlebum. I give him a position at one of my swing stations, and now he wants to ride shotgun messenger for me aboard one of my stages, which at one time or another could be carrying a considerable quantity of gold or specie. With a man I don't know I could gamble out at a lonely swing station, but sitting on the box of a stage, I'd have to think twice. Do you follow me, Mulvane?"

Grady was frowning. "You think I could be in with this holdup crowd?"

Lamonte shook his head. "I'm only asking you to put yourself in my position, Mulvane. Remember, I don't know you. No one in this town knew you until a few days ago."

The man was speaking sense, and Grady, grudgingly, had to concede this. Jim Lamonte was up against the wall, and he couldn't afford to take any chances with a stranger up on the box, who at one moment along the road could stick a gun into the driver's ribs and make off with the Wells Fargo box.

"I regret doing this," Lamonte said. "Maybe at a later date."

Grady nodded.

"I appreciate your good intentions, Mulvane," Lamonte assured him, and that was the end of the interview.

Before Grady left the office, a tall, slender man in black, with a thin, cavernous face, and deep-set hollow black eyes entered it. The man was introduced to Grady as Willets, the new Wells Fargo special agent.

Evidently, this man recognized the futility of posing as someone else. He'd come here for a particular reason, and he was letting men know about it. Grady wondered if this were not the better way to go about it, in view of the fact that the raids on the Lamonte stages were undoubtedly planned by someone on the inside.

"You will cooperate with Mr. Willets in every way," Lamonte told Grady before he left. "If he needs fresh horses, see to it that he gets the best out at Elder Creek."

"We'll work with him," Grady nodded. "Luck," he said to Willets, and the thin man nodded without expression.

Grady was not too much impressed with Willets, until he got a glimpse of the man's gun and holster underneath the black coat. It made a difference. There was nothing fancy about the gun, or about the holster. The gun was a standard Colt .44, and the holster of black leather, but very soft and very pliable. It was worn rather low on Willets' hip, also, which was another sign that the man knew how to use it.

Outside, loosening the gray from the tie rail, Grady saw Ben Champion coming up.

"Just left you," the sheriff smiled. "You follow me in?"

Grady told him of his meeting with Judith, and then Lace Madison, and of his decision to ask Lamonte if he could ride messenger on his stages.

"Jim could use a man like you," Ben nodded in agreement.

Grady looked at him across the tie rail. "He turned me down," he said, and he saw the sheriff's blue eyes widen.

"Jim turned you down?"

Grady nodded. "Figured he didn't know me well enough to let me ride shotgun," he said.

A brief shadow came into Ben Champion's eyes for a moment, but he only frowned and said, "Reckon that's Jim's decision."

Grady said to him, "Meet the new Wells Fargo man? He's inside."

Champion looked toward the depot door. "He got here pretty quick," he murmured. "I'll see him."

That shadow still was on Ben Champion's face, though, when he left Grady and walked toward the stage depot.

It was well after dark when Grady reached Elder Creek, and Tom O'Hara had already made his supper and was sitting out on the bench in front of the shack smoking his pipe.

"You took a hell of a long time lookin' for that horse," O'Hara observed, "an' then you come back without him." He added, "Beans an' sowbelly on the stove, an' plenty of coffee."

"I went in to Bottle Springs to see Lamonte about a new job," Grady explained as he passed in through the door.

"Too quiet here?" O'Hara called after him.

106

"I wanted to ride shotgun," Grady told him. "He turned me down."

Outside, Tom O'Hara considered this fact while Grady ladled some of the beans into a plate and then reached for the coffee pot.

"Why'd he turn you down?" O'Hara asked when Grady came out with his plate and coffee and sat down on the bench.

"Figured he couldn't trust me, yet."

Tom O'Hara didn't say anything to that. He looked at the ground, he looked up at the crescent moon swinging up over the distant low hills, and then he entered the shack.

"You figure he should have signed me on?" Grady said, smiling.

The old man shrugged. "Jim Lamonte runs this outfit," he observed. "Reckon if he says no, that's it, mister."

He said no more on the subject, but Grady knew he was in deep thought because usually the man would have a lot more questions to ask.

"Ran into Lace Madison outside of Bottle Springs," Grady said. "He was kind of keeping Judith Lamonte in sight when she was out riding."

"You saw her, too," O'Hara murmured. "You get around, boy."

"He making a play for Miss Lamonte?" Grady asked.

"Miss Lamonte," O'Hara scowled, "an' every other pretty gal from here to Sherman City an' back."

"How does he get along with Ben Champion?"

"Ben don't like him," O'Hara said promptly. "Told me so, himself."

Grady ate his beans and bacon and drank the coffee, and then O'Hara said to him, "Now there's three of you sparkin' Miss Lamonte."

"Who do you pick?" Grady smiled.

"Champion," O'Hara told him. "Lace Madison next, an' you last."

"Maybe I can change that," Grady said, and he wasn't smiling.

"An' maybe you can do better for yourself at the Diamond Stud," O'Hara observed. "That is, if you wasn't such a damned fool."

"Lorna Greene?" Grady asked. "Would you take her?"

"If I was your age," O'Hara chuckled, "an' the marryin' kind, I'd take her an' to hell with what anybody said. There's a woman stands on her own feet. Don't ask favors from nobody."

"She's too damned independent," Grady scowled.

"An' your kind," O'Hara told him.

Grady Mulvane didn't believe this, but he went to sleep that night thinking about it, and he decided that Tom O'Hara was wrong. His interest in Lorna Greene right from the start was out of pity, and nothing more.

Willets, the Wells Fargo man, came through the next morning, riding the westbound, and he had a few words with Grady and O'Hara as they were changing the teams. He apparently was a man of few words, but when he had gone on, O'Hara said thoughtfully,

"Reckon they won't bring that one back on the roof of a stage."

Grady had come to the same conclusion, but yet there were things he didn't like about Willets. The Wells Fargo man was a cold fish; he was not going about his job in a way calculated to get Lamonte Line employees behind him in his fight against the road agents. He gave the impression that he was not particularly interested in their support.

"He's a loner," O'Hara said. "Hate to have him against me."

Willets rode off in the stage, and Grady noticed that this stage didn't have a messenger on the box with the driver. Very possibly, Willets was inviting a raid on the stage, and he would be ready for them with that Colt on his hip.

Grady rolled a cigarette and watched the big Concord roll out onto the flats along Elder Creek. He said thoughtfully, "Maybe this one will do it."

He wasn't sure, though. There was something about Willets which had not rung true.

CHAPTER
TEN

It was a week later when Willets came back through, and in that week there had been no raids on Lamonte Line. The following day a westbound on the other side of Flat Rock station was hit, and the Wells Fargo treasure chest taken. Ed Grubaker had been on the box, with Buck Neil riding messenger.

"That's it," Tom O'Hara growled when they heard the news. "That crowd waited till Willets got back into Bottle Springs. Now they're back in business."

"Wells Fargo man going out after them?" Grady asked the driver who had brought them the news.

"Ain't seen him around lately," the driver told them. "Cold duck, ain't he, though?"

Grady watered the teams which had just come in, and he was scowling as he brought up water from the creek. He said to Tom O'Hara when he came up with two pails, "How many times has Grubaker been hit when he was handling the reins?"

O'Hara thought for a moment. "Four," he said.

"What about Neil?"

The old man laughed grimly. "Don't figure Buck's fired his gun at 'em, yet," he stated. "Must be six times they hung it on Buck."

"Why does Jim Lamonte keep him on?" Grady demanded.

O'Hara looked at him. "I ain't Jim Lamonte," he said. Grady came back with more water, and then he had enough. "I'm riding in to Bottle Springs," he said.

"You're aimin' to get fired," O'Hara told him.

Grady smiled. "We'll see," he said.

He saddled the gray and rode the twelve miles to town, arriving in Bottle Springs a little past noon. He rode straight to the Lamonte office, and had to cool his heels for half an hour before Jim Lamonte arrived. He'd apparently been out to lunch with Willets, the Wells Fargo man, and Willets was with him now.

Both men looked at Grady curiously as they came in, and Lamonte said, "You want to see me, Mulvane?"

"Like to talk about that messenger job again," Grady told him.

Jim Lamonte frowned. Willets moved across the room toward the window, took a long, slender cigarillo from his coat pocket and put it into his mouth. He didn't light it, but he stood there with his back to the wall near the window, watching Grady, saying nothing.

"I thought," Lamonte said, a little ruffled, "that we'd settled that."

"Your stages are still being hit," Grady stated, "and you've got a man like Neil, who never uses the shotgun on the box."

Willets said softly from across the room, "You figure you'd use it, mister?"

Grady looked at him. "I'd use it," he said. "I want the chance to use it."

"I'm not firing Neil," Lamonte said. "He's been with the outfit a long time. I'm satisfied that these road agents have had the drop on him."

"Six times?" Grady asked.

Jim Lamonte's lean, white face became tense, and his dark eyes seemed to recede into his head. "Don't you like your job out at Elder Creek?" he asked.

Grady took a deep breath. "I like to work for an outfit which will fight back at the dogs who are trying to destroy it," he said.

"You don't think I'm trying to fight back?"

"Are you?" Grady demanded.

Jim Lamonte looked out the window. "I'll send a new man out to Elder Creek," he said. "You're through, Mulvane."

"I'll finish out the month," Grady snapped. "You've paid me for that."

He turned and walked out of the office. He had intended to ride straight back to Elder Creek, but coming out on the street he caught a glimpse of Ed Grubaker entering the Diamond Stud.

Leading the gray in that direction, he tied up outside the gambling house and went in. Grubaker was there, in conversation with Lace Madison at the far end of the bar, and both men turned to look at him as he pushed in through the batwing doors.

At this hour of the day there were less than half a dozen people in the house, and Grady figured that half of these could be professional gamblers who worked in the establishment, and who were now whiling away

112

these afternoon hours until the games started up in the evening.

Buck Neil, the shotgun messenger, was at a corner table playing solitaire, and he stared at Grady, hatred in his eyes.

Grady pulled up at the bar and ordered a drink, and then Madison came down toward him, smiling, but his eyes were a shade bluer than Grady had seen them before. Possibly Lace Madison was remembering that Grady had spoiled his rendezvous with Judith Lamonte.

Madison said, "Back in town again?"

Grady said sourly, "Your job to check up on me, or sell liquor?"

"If you can pay," Madison told him, "I'll sell you the whisky."

Grady slapped a coin down on the bar. It was one of the last he had, and it didn't bother him, even though there would be no more coming when he finished his month at Elder Creek.

"Hear they're still raiding Lamonte stages," Madison said.

"You hear right," Grady told him.

"Still figure you'd like to ride shotgun?"

He was grinning at Grady, and it was almost as if he were taunting him.

"Lamonte just fired me because I wanted to ride shotgun," Grady told him. "That please you?"

Lace Madison nodded. "You had it coming," he said. "A big mouth and empty pockets."

"This holster's not empty," Grady said, and he patted his gunbelt.

Lace Madison's grin broadened and he shook his head. "You don't get me into a gunfight," he chuckled. "Why the hell should I be shot down by a drifter who's out of work and hasn't got a nickel to his name? No profit in it."

"Tell him off, Lace," Buck Neil said from the corner.

Grady looked over at him. "You tell me, Buck," he said.

Neil looked at Madison, and then at Grubaker at the other end of the bar, and then he wiped his mouth with the back of his hand. He didn't make any move to get up, and he watched Grady lift his glass to his mouth.

"You're a tough one," Lace Madison commented, "but we've handled tough ones before."

It was a slip of the tongue, and immediately after saying it, Grady could see that he would have given a thousand dollars to be able to take it back. The remark indicated clearly that he and Neil, and probably Grubaker, were working together on something, and that something could mean only one thing. Tom O'Hara thought Madison knew something about the raids on the Lamonte stages, and both Neil and Grubaker, Lamonte employees, were invariably looking the other way when the road agents struck.

Grady gave no indication that he'd noticed anything amiss about Madison's remark. He said simply, "Reckon you've never handled me before, mister." He deliberately taunted the man now, hoping he'd forget

114

himself and make another remark which would definitely align him with Grubaker and Neil.

"Finish your drink," Lace Madison said, "and get outside. You're not welcome here any more, mister."

"Don't try to rush me," Grady warned him, and he took his time, smiling at the three of them, and then Lace Madison looked over at Buck Neil, and Neil got up.

When he started moving toward the bar, Ed Grubaker stirred into action, also, and both men drew up alongside Lace Madison.

"You want some more, Ed?" Grady asked the stage driver.

"Maybe this time you'll get it," Grubaker murmured. "Reckon you been askin' for it a long time."

"You won't do it alone," Grady told him, "and you'll get about as much help from Neil as you get from him when the road agents hit your stage."

Lace Madison said four words softly, and he wasn't giving a damn what Grady thought of them, or made of them.

"Out in the alley," Madison said.

Grubaker took a step forward, and then Lorna Greene came jauntily down the stairs. This was daytime, and she was dressed to go out. She wore a little straw hat with a feather in it, and she was humming as she came down the stairs.

Seeing Grady at the bar, she steered that way immediately, her brown eyes lighting up. "Waiting for me long?" she said, and smiled, and took his arm, steering him toward the door.

For one moment Grady was tempted to pull away from her, and see what Ed Grubaker and Buck Neil could do to him in the alley, but it would have been an act of foolishness. Two good-sized men could always lick one man no matter how tough he was, and there was the possibility Lace Madison might take a hand in this, also, not to mention the bartender behind them, who would be equipped with a sawed-off pool cue.

They went out the door together and started up the street toward the stores at the other end of town, and Grady said, "Your hearing is very good. How long were you listening in?"

"Long enough to know what was going on. Why did you do it?"

Grady shrugged. "Why did you do it?" he asked.

"I don't like to see a man beaten," she said, "and, besides, you helped me out at Elder Cheek, and you've tried to help in other ways."

"They'd have had a time beating me," Grady mused.

Her hand was still on his arm as they walked along, and it was still there when Judith Lamonte came out of a drygoods store a few doors up from them, and came in their direction.

Seeing Judith, Grady was tempted to take Lorna's hand from his arm, but it was already too late, and he felt a little wave of anger running over him as Judith saw them, her eyes lifting slightly in surprise.

Lorna Greene seemed to read Grady's mind, because she let her hand slip down as Grady touched his hat to the girl. They passed on, and Lorna said gravely, "She's not for you, Grady. You're wasting your time."

"I didn't ask you," Grady reminded her.

They paused out in front of a store, and Grady looked down at her.

"You're rough," Lorna said, "and you're hard, and after a while it would tell on her. Ben Champion's her man."

"You know everything," Grady snapped.

"Remember that I said it," Lorna told him, and she walked past him into the store.

In a bad mood, Grady walked on till he came to Ben Champion's office, and seeing the door open, he stepped inside.

The sheriff of Bottle Springs was leaning back in his swivel chair, a small yellow cat in his lap. He looked up and smiled as Grady came in.

"What brings you to town?" he asked.

"I'm through out at Elder Creek," Grady told him, and he watched the frown come to the sheriff's face.

"Trouble?" Champion asked.

Grady told him of his talk with Jim Lamonte, and Ben Champion let the yellow cat slide to the floor as he listened.

"Why the hell does he keep men like Grubaker and Neil?" Grady demanded. "Neil hasn't fired a shot since he's riding messenger for him."

Ben Champion said nothing about that. He sat in his swivel chair, moving it gently from side to side, and staring at the floor.

"Few minutes ago," Grady went on, "they were ready to jump me in the Diamond Stud, and Lace Madison was egging them on. I figure Madison knows more than a little about these raids, too."

Champion looked at him. "How about proof?" he asked.

"Hard to prove anything," Grady growled.

"And you're finished with Lamonte Line after the end of the month. What'll you do?"

Grady shrugged. "Push on," he said. He knew that he didn't particularly want to push on, after having met Judith Lamonte. "In the meanwhile," he added thoughtfully, "I can keep my eyes open."

"Stay away from Madison," Champion warned. "He can be a bad one."

"He can't drive me," Grady said.

"You've crossed him," Champion scowled, "and he won't forget it."

"I won't forget it, either." Grady smiled grimly.

He stayed for a few minutes with Champion, and then he left. He had to return to the Diamond Stud for the gray which he'd left at the tie-rail.

Buck Neil and Ed Grubaker were waiting for him out on the porch, knowing that he'd have to come back. Neil spat across the walk as Grady approached, and he said, "Reckon you were a little lucky before, Mulvane."

"Finish it now," Grady challenged.

Neil nodded toward the alley to the right of the gambling house.

118

Grady looked for Lace Madison, but didn't see him. He said, "Come in one at a time if you want it. If you both come in at once, I'll shoot you down."

Neil grinned and said to Grubaker, "Reckon you can finish up with him when I get through, Ed."

The statement should have warned Grady, because Buck Neil had not been too pugnacious before, and he'd shut up when Grady put the pressure on him. Now he apparently was itching for a fight, and willing to go it alone.

Grady looked at him, and then walked toward the alley. At this early afternoon hour the streets were very quiet, most people remaining indoors because of the heat.

The alley separating the Diamond Stud from a rundown saddlemaker's shop on the other side could not have been more than eight or ten feet wide, and it ran the length of the building, another sixty feet.

Stepping into the alley, Grady felt the cool air. He walked halfway down the alley, looking back over his shoulder as he walked, not quite sure what Neil was going to do, and half expecting him to draw a gun and open up with it.

Neil came after him, moving slowly, grinning, and the grin should have warned Grady, too, but it didn't. To prove to Grady that he did not have gunplay in mind, he unbuckled the gunbelt as he walked, and placed it carefully on the ground against the wall of the building.

Halfway down the alley, Grady stopped and unbuckled his own belt. He placed it on the ground, and he was straightening up when the roof of the Diamond Stud apparently hit him on the back of the head.

He stumbled forward, reaching for the ground with his hands, and even as he fell he saw Buck Neil running toward him, pale blue eyes glittering, fists clenched.

He was clubbed a second time from behind, probably with that sawed-off cue stick, and he knew then that he'd made his mistake by coming in here, and he was going to pay for it.

Buck Neil's boot was coming at his face, and he managed to turn his head slightly to avoid the full force of the kick, but the sharp toe of the boot caught him on the cheek, laying his cheek open, and as his face fell forward into the dirt, he saw Ed Grubaker running into the alley. He remembered that Grubaker owed him something, too, and Grubaker intended to pay it back.

CHAPTER
ELEVEN

The two blows on the back of the head by the unknown assailant had stunned Grady badly, and Buck Neil's first kick nearly finished the job, but Grady was dimly aware before the blackness closed in around him that there were three men scuffling around him, kicking and stamping, and he was sure he heard Lace Madison's voice.

He never knew how long they'd worked over him, but they'd done a good job of it, and no one happened by the alley opening before they were finished with him.

It was a little boy of ten who found him an hour or more later. The boy came strolling down the alley hitting at a tin can with a stick, and he took one look at Grady's bloodied face, let out a yell, and raced down the street to bump into Ben Champion, who was just emerging from his office.

Ben, with the help of another passerby, got him up to a room at the hotel, summoned Doc Watson, and then at a loss as to what to do next, got Lorna Greene from the Diamond Stud.

Grady regained consciousness as Lorna was applying damp cloths to his bruised face. Doc Watson had worked on the worst cuts, cleaning them, and grumbling to himself as he did so. Ben Champion was still there, standing with his hat in his hand near the window, his face tense. Champion came to the foot of the bed when Grady opened his right eye; the left one was swollen shut.

Champion said to him, "Reckon you've had it, Grady."

Grady nodded his head slightly.

"See them?"

Again Grady nodded, and he looked at Lorna Greene this time.

"I brought her over," Champion explained. "You'll need somebody to look after you a bit."

"No ribs broken," Doc Watson said as he packed his bag. "You're damned lucky, mister. Looked like your sides were kicked by a horse."

Grady lay there, looking up at the ceiling with the one good eye, remembering what had happened in that alley, knowing what he had to do about it. He felt now the way he'd felt when he'd come back to the shack out in the foothills of the Rockies, and he'd found his horses gone, his place burned, and his partner dead. He'd had to repay that, too, and he would have traveled ten thousand miles to do it.

He felt the pain in his face, in his sides, at the base of the skull. Looking up at Lorna Greene, he realized what he must have looked like when they brought him in here.

"Neil and Grubaker?" Champion asked.

122

Grady didn't say anything. He lay looking up at the ceiling, and he heard Champion give a grunt of annoyance.

"You'll go gunning for them," he said, "and maybe you'll kill them, and that will make you happy."

"Let it go," Grady mumbled.

His lips were swollen and split and he could feel that a few of his front teeth were loose, which prevented him from speaking properly. The voice did not sound like his own voice. He said to Lorna, "Madison will fire you for this."

"Was Madison in on it?" she asked. "He was pushing them in the Diamond Stud."

"I didn't see Madison," Grady murmured. He was positive, though, that he'd heard the man, and if so it could mean that Madison was the one who'd used the club on him from behind.

Doc Watson said, "Stay in bed for a day or two. You'll be stiff for a week."

"I'll be up in an hour," Grady told him.

"You won't," Lorna Greene promised.

Grady looked at her and said nothing. Doc Watson left the room, and Ben Champion said, "I'll have some supper sent up. You feel like eating?"

"Coffee," Grady said. He came up on his elbows and he lay there, scowling. They'd stripped off his bloody shirt, and he was naked to the waist. He could see his ribs when the sheet fell back a little. He was bruised and purple right down to the belt line.

"You don't want to talk about it," Champion said.

"It's my fight," Grady told him briefly.

"I'm the law in this town," Champion observed.

"Protect the women and children," Grady said.

Ben Champion frowned at him, and then left the room. Grady said to the girl, "You're working tonight. Better get back to the Diamond Stud."

"Madison was in it, wasn't he?" she said. "He wanted them to get you in the alley before."

"Maybe he was in it," Grady growled. "You're not."

"I won't be going back," Lorna Greene said. "I wouldn't work for a man like that."

"You're losing your job on account of me," Grady snapped. "Don't be a damned fool."

"You didn't want me to work there in the first place," Lorna pointed out.

Grady didn't say anything to that.

They sat there for a while in silence, and then she said, "You're going to kill them, aren't you?"

"Sooner or later," Grady mumbled, "everybody dies."

"Madison has a lot of friends in this town. If you kill him, they'll never let you leave Bottle Springs alive."

"Would that bother you?" Grady asked her.

"Yes," she said.

Then she bent down and kissed his battered lips. "You're the only good man I've ever met," she said. "The others were trash. That's why I took the chance of coming here. You don't know how down a woman can get, Grady, a woman alone in the world."

"If you'd married that nester," Grady observed, "you'd surely have been down. I passed his place. You'd have been a work horse."

124

"I suppose I should say, then, that I'm glad he's dead."

"Why did you kiss me?" Grady asked.

"For your goodness," she said, "for your foolishness, your recklessness, for a lot of things." She added slowly, "But you're in love with Judith Lamonte. She's a fine girl. She came to see me one afternoon, and she's invited me to tea. She's too good to be true, Grady, but she's not for you."

"Who's for me?" Grady asked bitterly. "Look at my face, and I'm flat broke, and without a job."

"You'll come out of that," Lorna smiled. "You're a driver, Grady. You'll go where you want to go."

Ben Champion came in with the coffee. He carried a pot and two cups, and he said to Lorna, "You'll be staying around for a while?"

"Yes," she nodded.

"Then why not go down and have your supper," he told her. "Reckon I'll sit here for a spell."

"Why?" Grady asked him.

Champion smiled. "You know damned well why. They might decide to come back and finish you up."

"If they'd wanted to finish me," Grady pointed out, "they could have done it in the alley."

Champion shrugged. "Maybe they thought they had finished you. You looked it when I picked you up out of that alley."

Grady looked around the drab little hotel room. He said, "Who's paying for this?"

"Pay me back when your luck turns," Champion murmured.

Grady frowned. "Been a hell of a summer," he said. "Lamonte know I'm laid up here?"

"I told him," Ben nodded. "I said you'd likely be headed out to Elder Creek when you felt up to it."

"That'll be in the morning," Grady told him.

Ben Champion poured coffee for the both of them, and he handed Grady a cup as he sat up in bed.

"Grubaker or Neil in town?" Grady asked him.

"Haven't seen them," Champion said. "Reckon they'll lay low for a while."

"What about Madison?"

"He's at his bar," Champion said. "Forget about him."

"Like hell," Grady said over the rim of his cup. He noticed that Champion had draped his gunbelt over the foot of the bed, and he said, "Hand me the gun, Ben."

Ben Champion slipped the gun out of the holster and handed it to him, butt first. "Why?" he asked.

"They might come again," Grady smiled. "Remember?"

He had another cup of coffee after slipping the gun under the pillow behind him, and he felt a lot better.

"My advice to you," Champion said, "is to get to hell out to Elder Creek tomorrow and rest up a few days. You'll look worse tomorrow, but after that it'll start to get better."

"I'm not tackling anybody just yet," Grady said wryly.

Lorna Greene came back, in a short while, and Ben Champion put on his hat and picked up the empty coffee pot and the cups.

"I'll keep an eye on this place," he said.

126

"They come in here," Grady told him, "and they're dead." When Champion had gone out, Grady said to the girl, "You tell Madison you were through?"

"I told him," she nodded.

"And now what will you do?"

"We'll see what happens," she smiled. "It's not the first time I didn't have any plans."

He looked around the room, and frowned, and said, "You can't stay here tonight."

"I've taken a room down the hall," she said. "When you want me to go, I'll go. If you want anything, you can call me. I'll leave my door open."

Grady scowled up at the ceiling. "Why are you doing this?" he asked.

Lorna Greene looked down at him steadily. "I think because I love you, Grady," she said.

Grady Mulvane took a deep breath, and then he said slowly, "That's a hell of a thing. A real hell of a thing."

She went out, and came back in a little while with a kettle of hot water she'd gotten in the hotel kitchen, and she poured the water into a basin, and then she applied hot towels to his battered face.

"Doctor Watson said it would take some of the swelling down," she explained, "particularly around the eyes."

Grady lay there, eyes closed, thinking of the time he'd been a lot worse off than this, when a tough bronc had thrown him, and he'd been laid up in a dreary bunkhouse with a broken cheekbone and a broken arm, and there had been no one around to see to his needs except toughened riders like himself who came and went. It was good having a woman around at a time like this.

"Feel better?" she asked.

"It feels better." Grady nodded, and then there was a knock on the door, and he reached under his pillow for the Colt gun, sliding it out, and holding it in his hand under the sheet over him.

Lorna went to answer the door, and when she opened it, Judith Lamonte stood there. She did not seem surprised at seeing Lorna there, and Grady realized that either Ben Champion or her brother had informed her that Lorna was looking after him.

"Can I do anything?" Judith asked Lorna.

"I guess Grady would like to see you," Lorna smiled. "Come in."

Judith came over to the bed. She was wearing a shawl over her head, and a light cape over her shoulders because the night had turned cool after the heat of the day.

"I'm very sorry about this, Grady," she almost apologized. "I'm sure Jim will do everything he can to punish the men who did it. They were Lamonte Line men, weren't they?"

"Grubaker and Neil," Grady nodded. "I invited one at a time to come into the alley, but they jumped me, along with, another one."

He didn't tell her that he was positive Lace Madison had been the third man in that alley, wielding a club on him.

"I don't suppose there is much I can do," Judith was saying. "You're very fortunate in having Miss Greene around."

128

Grady nodded. "Glad you dropped in," he said. "Tell your brother I expect to ride out to Elder Creek tomorrow."

"There's no haste," she assured him. "Jim wouldn't want you to go back to work if you weren't well."

He knew, then, that her brother hadn't told her that he'd fired his new station man, and he wondered if he ought to tell her. He decided to let it ride. She'd find out soon enough.

He had his opportunity here to compare the two girls, and it was the first time he'd ever really seen them together, and he was surprised that Lorna did not show up to disadvantage. She was not quite as tall as Judith, and several years older. She no longer had the fresh bloom on her, but she was a fine-looking woman, brown-haired where Judith's hair was black. The features, though, were not unpleasant, and he was thinking that she was a lot prettier than he'd first imagined when she'd gotten off at Elder Creek station.

Judith was looking around the room now, and Lorna said easily, "I have a room down the hall. I've left my job at the Diamond Stud."

"That's nice," Judith smiled. She didn't say whether it was nice that Lorna had a room down the hall, or that she'd left her job at the Diamond Stud. "If there's anything I can do," she said, "don't hesitate to call on me."

"I'm obliged for your coming," Grady murmured.

When she left the room, Lorna said gently, "You would have liked it better if I had not been here. You're a fool, Grady."

"All right," Grady said. "All right."

He was in a bad mood, and it was not all because Grubaker and Buck Neil had worked him over. He had other things on his mind, many things.

CHAPTER
TWELVE

In the morning Lorna knocked gently on his door, but he was already dressed and looking at his battered face in the mirror. The eye which had been closed was beginning to open now, but his mouth was puffed, and the gash on his cheekbone had swollen the left side of his face far out of proportion.

"You feel any better?" Lorna asked him.

"Reckon I'm all right," Grady nodded.

"I've ordered breakfast for you downstairs," she said, "whenever you're ready to come down."

Grady was remembering that he had no money in his pockets with which to pay for a breakfast, or for anything else. He said gruffly, "I'll be eating out at Elder Creek."

She handed him a few bills, and he looked at them, shaking his head, the color coming to his face. It was the first time a woman had ever offered him money.

"Not from me," she smiled. "Mr. Champion said you could use it until you got another job."

Grady took the money, then, remembering that once again he was indebted to the sheriff.

"You sure you're well enough to ride?" Lorna asked him.

"I'll ride," Grady assured her.

His body was stiff from the bruises, but he was sure riding would take some of that out of him.

Strapping on his gunbelt, and taking his hat from a peg on the wall, he went downstairs with Lorna. They had breakfast in the empty dining room.

She said, when they'd finished, "Now you're going to kill someone?"

"They'll be gone," Grady told her, "but I'll run into them."

He was a little awkward about leaving her, because she'd been good to him, and he said as he got up, "You'll be staying in Bottle Springs?"

"For a while," she nodded. "I may be able to find other work. I'm looking now."

"I'd help," Grady said, "if I could."

"I know you would." She smiled up at him.

"And I'm obliged to you for looking after me."

"I was glad to do it," she said. As he touched his hat to her, she said, "Please be careful. You're no good to anybody dead."

"I'll be careful," Grady promised.

He left the hotel and crossed to the Diamond Stud, and he pushed in through the batwing doors to look around the empty gambling house. It was not yet ten o'clock in the morning and there were no customers. The bar was empty, and a swamper was pushing sawdust around with a broom. Then the bartender whom Grady had seen the day before came out of a back room. He stared at Grady for a moment, saying

132

nothing, and Grady said to him, "Grubaker or Neil around?"

"No," the bartender said.

Lace Madison wasn't around, either, and Grady wondered what he would have done if he'd seen Madison in the room. He still wasn't as positive about Madison as he was about Grubaker and Neil, although Madison had been involved in the matter.

Leaving the Diamond Stud, Grady started up the street, conscious of the fact that people were watching him. Ben Champion had stabled his gray somewhere, and he would have to see Ben, but first he headed for the Lamonte Line yard where it was possible Grubaker and Neil would be.

A blacksmith in one of the shops looked up at him as he was shoeing a horse, dropped the horse's foot to stare at Grady's face, and then said that neither Grubaker nor Neil had been in the yard that morning.

A man he hadn't expected to meet was standing at the back door of the Lamonte Line office when he swung past, and Grady slowed down, nodding to him.

Willets, the Wells Fargo agent, nodded back and said, "You run into a buzz saw, mister?"

He had a soft, purring voice with a slight Southern accent to it, and watching him Grady got the peculiar feeling that the man was deriding him.

"The men I'm looking for," he said, "will wish a buzz saw had worked on them."

Willets nodded. "You're a hard one," he said. "Luck."

Grady passed on to the street, and then walked down to Ben Champion's office. Ben had apparently heard that he was up and about, and was now looking for him. They met out in front of the Cheyenne Saloon.

"You gunning for somebody already?" Ben asked grimly.

"What would you do?" Grady asked him.

"I'd wait till I could see out of both eyes, at least," Champion growled. "I'd have that much patience."

"You're not me," Grady told him, "and it didn't happen to you." He added, "I'm obliged for the loan. I'm always owing you something." He wondered what he would owe Ben Champion if he took his girl away from him.

"Grubaker and Neil are gone," Champion said. "I heard they skipped town last night. Best thing for you is to head out to Elder Creek and rest up now."

"Figured I'd do that," Grady nodded. "You stable my horse?"

"Down at the Emerald Corral," Champion said. "Paid for."

Grady winced a little. "I owe you plenty," he said. "I'll stay around to pay it back."

"Forget it."

Grady rode on out to Elder Creek, and he found Tom O'Hara currying one of the horses when he came into the yard. O'Hara took a good look at him and then put down his brush. He watched Grady dismount stiffly before saying anything, and then he said, "Reckon there was more than one of 'em worked on you, Grady, an' they didn't use only their fists."

134

Grady tried to smile, but his battered face hurt and he gave it up. He walked stiffly to the bench and sat down.

"Grubaker an' Neil," O'Hara said shrewdly, "an' maybe a few more of 'em thrown in."

"Right so far," Grady nodded.

"They dead, yet?"

"Not yet," Grady said.

"Best to stay the hell away from town," O'Hara told him. "Only find trouble for yourself."

"Reckon I'm through out here, too," Grady smiled, "after the end of the month."

He told the old man of his talk with Jim Lamonte, and of Lamonte's reaction, and O'Hara was frowning when he finished.

"Line will go to hell that way," the old man said. "Jim Lamonte's no stage man."

Grady knew that, too, and he was wondering now why the Wells Fargo man didn't see it and put a little pressure on Lamonte. Willets had come here to stop the raids on the Wells Fargo boxes, and even a fool could see that the raids were successful largely because Lamonte Line was run on a very loose and easy basis.

"Next couple of days," O'Hara advised, "you just lay around here, Grady, until that face heals up. You're a hell of a sight."

"I'm paid to work here," Grady said. "I'll work."

"Stubborn as a mule." O'Hara grinned. "What'll you do if Grubaker and Neil are ridin' the box on the next stage through?"

"Reckon we'll see if they come," Grady murmured.

They would know he was out here at Elder Creek, and if they continued to work for Lamonte Line they would have to come through Elder Creek sooner or later. He wondered if they would come.

For the rest of the day Grady hauled water and worked on the gear, and he even rolled stones and helped Tom O'Hara raise the stone corral a bit higher, the old man protesting all the while and telling him to go sit in the shade.

A westbound coach went through, but neither Grubaker nor Neil was on the box. When Grady asked the driver if they were in town, he was vague about it, and Tom O'Hara said when the coach was gone, "Reckon they're somewhere close by, Grady, but that Grubaker's a rough one, an' there ain't too many boys crossin' him."

That evening Tom O'Hara boiled some herbs he'd gathered in the hills and made a concoction which he applied to the cuts, bruises and swellings on Grady's face.

"Kiowas taught me this," O'Hara explained. "Used to know some of 'em years ago. Best thing I ever heard of for takin' the swelling down."

The lotion was good, and Grady felt considerably better. Both his eyes were open, and while he still bore plenty of black and purple marks, the stiffness had gone out of him.

In the morning Ben Champion showed up. Apparently he had something on his mind, and a matter which was not pleasant. For some time he sat out in front of the

136

shack with Grady smoking, saying little, and then he came out with it.

"You met Willets, the new Wells Fargo man?"

"I met him," Grady nodded.

"What do you think?"

"He's a cold one," Grady said, "and he's tough."

"More than that," Champion growled. "He's a fake."

Grady stared at him. "Fake?" he repeated.

"He's not a Wells Fargo man," Champion said quietly. "I wired Wells Fargo's Chicago office. They haven't sent a new man out this way yet."

Grady rubbed his jaw. "Reckon that'll make Willets one of this crowd," he murmured. "That the way you look at it, Ben? Maybe the head man."

"He'll be one of them," Champion nodded. "I don't know who the hell the head man is. Maybe we can find out today. Lamonte's shipping at least thirty or forty thousand in the Wells Fargo treasure on the westbound this morning, due through here in an hour. I found that out, too."

"They'll hit it," Grady murmured, "and you aim to be there when it happens."

"I rode east out of Bottle Springs this morning," Ben told him. "I let it be known that I was headed back to Wind Junction. I circled the town, then, and rode out this way. Figured you might like to be in on this, Grady."

"I'm in it," Grady nodded.

"Even after Lamonte fired you?"

"I'm working for Lamonte till the end of the month. What is it you have in mind, Ben?"

"I figure to be close by when that stage is stopped, and it'll be stopped, but I won't be close enough. A man riding in the rear boot could be a lot closer, and it wouldn't take anything to crawl inside just as they're leaving here."

"I'll do it," Grady told him. "If Lace Madison is in this, I owe him one, and Grubaker and Neil, too."

Ben Champion nodded. "I'll be moving parallel with the road," he said, "and keeping out of sight. If you'll start it, I'll be in at the finish. It'll take somebody to start it."

"I'll start it," Grady assured him. "Who'll be up on the box?"

"New man," Champion said. "I don't know him. He could be in with them." He added, "I'll take one of your horses along. We might have to go after them."

"Take my gray," Grady told him.

Tom O'Hara, who had been listening, said morosely, "They'll shoot the hell out of you, before Champion can come up."

Ben Champion said to Grady, "I'm not asking you to start anything unless you figure you have a pretty good chance of finishing it with my help. If there are too many of them, lay low until it's over, and then drop out of the boot when you start up again, and wait for me with the horses."

"We'll see," Grady murmured.

The sheriff of Bottle Springs looked at him for a moment, and then frowned.

"You figure you owe somebody something?" he asked.

"You know it," Grady nodded. "Reckon I'd pay it back one way or another. This way I'm helping Lamonte Line."

Ben Champion had to accept it that way. He handed Grady a star and swore him in as deputy to make it legal, and then he rode off when they sighted the dust of the westbound just behind Dutchman's Ridge. He took the gray with him.

Tom O'Hara said, "You're buyin' a one-way ticket, mister."

Grady shrugged. He'd lain awake for a long time last night thinking things over. He was nearly twenty-eight now, and he wasn't going anywhere, and he was flat broke. Most of his twenty-eight years the cards had been going against him, like the wild-horse deal with Joe Beauford. He had his chance here to do somebody some good. Even though Jim Lamonte had fired him, Lamonte had tried to set him on his feet; he owed it to Ben Champion to lend him a hand here. And maybe he owed something to Judith, too. She'd been kind to him; she hadn't looked upon him as a drifter.

If he didn't come back from this one, it would be too bad, but no one would be particularly affected. Except, he remembered, Lorna Greene, who had honestly told him that she loved him. He had respect for her, but respect was not love. He wondered if she would grieve if they brought him back on the roof of one of Lamonte's stages.

That was the one thing on his mind as he strapped on his gunbelt and waited for the westbound to come in to the yard.

CHAPTER
THIRTEEN

There were two men up on the box when the westbound rolled up, and Grady Mulvane was surprised to see that the man riding shotgun was Willets, the fake Wells Fargo agent. This fact apparently Ben Champion hadn't known, either. It meant that Willets and his crowd were going to make sure that the raid was successful.

The driver was a man Grady had never seen before, a squat, moon-faced man with a harelip. Both men remained up on the box as Grady and Tom O'Hara moved up to the lead horses to take them out of the traces, and then Grady stopped as he was passing the stage window. Lorna Greene was looking out at him, smiling.

He stared at her for a moment, and then he let Tom O'Hara take the horses and went over to the window. She was sitting at the rear seat, and Willets, up on the box, couldn't see or hear Grady when he spoke to her in a low voice.

There were two other passengers in the coach, both men, one of them elderly, and dozing on his seat.

"Where are you going?" Grady asked.

140

"I have a job in Sherman City," she said. "Judith Lamonte told me of a woman who needed help in her dress shop there."

Grady glanced up toward the box, and he said softly, "Step down. Go over to the house for a drink of water."

Lorna looked at him for a moment, and then nodded without a word. When Grady walked away to help O'Hara, he noticed that she was opening the door, and a few moments later he saw her up at the shack by the water bucket, taking a dipperful of water from the bucket.

Willets call down to Grady when they went by with the two wheelers, "Face looks a lot better, Mulvane."

Grady nodded. When he glanced toward the shack he noticed that Lorna was looking around for a glass or cup out of which she could drink, and she was thus giving him a reason for going back there.

He went back to the shack and got a clean cup for her, and he said as she poured the water into it, "Ben Champion figures this stage is being held up. They're carrying a big load of currency in, the Wells Fargo chest."

Lorna drank the water, looking at him over the rim of the cup. When she lowered the cup, she said, "They haven't been bothering the passengers."

"This time it'll be different," Grady scowled. "I'll be hiding in the rear boot of this stage when it pulls out, and Ben Champion will be following it. There'll be gunplay if the raiders hit us."

Lorna smiled at him. "I always carry a derringer," she said. "What can I do?"

141

"Wish you'd get off here," Grady scowled, "but if you do, it might scare them away. Man up on the box is one of them. Thin man in black."

"I'll just have to ride on, then," Lorna told him. "Be careful, yourself." She nodded her thanks for the water, and walked back to the stage. Tom O'Hara opened the door for her, and gave her a hand back in.

Grady moved around to the rear of the stage on his way up to help O'Hara with the swing team, and he noticed that the canvas flap was loose on the rear boot. Lifting it quickly, he saw several small mailbags inside, but there was still room for a man to slip inside and lower the flap again.

He helped O'Hara with the last team, and then he went back to stand near the rear wheel as the driver kicked his brake loose and lifted his whip. When the coach wheels started to move, Grady darted forward, lifted the canvas flap over the boot, and slid inside.

He lay in the darkness, holding his breath as the stage rolled along, wheels squeaking. If it stopped, it meant that one of the two men on the box had looked back, and seeing only one man where two had been standing, had become suspicious.

The coach continued to roll out on to the road, and Grady relaxed, positive now that he had not been seen. He worked his body around until his head came to rest on one of the mail sacks. He tried to make himself as comfortable as possible, not knowing how long he would have to remain in these cramped quarters. With the flap down it was hot and musty inside the boot, but he made the best of it. He'd worked his gun out of the

142

holster, and he lay with it in his lap now, ready for use at any moment.

It was impossible to tell when the raiders would strike. They'd never hit at any of the Lamonte stages so close to Bottle Springs, and it could, therefore, mean that he'd have a long ride ahead of him. He wondered how long he'd be able to ride in here without being detected. Attendants at the various swing and home stations did not usually bother to look inside the rear boot, and the mail wouldn't be taken out until they reached Sherman City, the last stop. It was three days to Sherman City, but Grady was positive the raiders would strike quickly, especially with Willets up on the box and a big haul to be made.

The next swing station beyond Elder Creek was High Mound, and Grady remembered Tom O'Hara telling him that a grumpy Swede by the name of Jorgens ran the place.

When they rolled into the High Mound yard, Willets got down from the box. Inside the boot, Grady could hear the man talking with Jorgens, commenting on the weather, and then asking him where he could get water.

He heard Willets walking past the boot, and he held his breath, wondering what he would do if Willets for any reason suddenly pulled the canvas flap up and looked inside.

Willets went on, though, and in a few minutes the new horses were in the traces, and they were rolling again. Grady took a deep breath and relaxed. He wondered how close Ben Champion was, and how soon Champion could get into the fight if there was one.

The big Concord rolled on through the late afternoon hours. There were several more stops, and at each one Grady waited, gun in hand, but then the stage rolled on again and nothing happened.

It was nearly dark when the Concord slowed down, when they were less than four or fives miles beyond the last change of horses. There had been no challenge, and no shots, so this was not the place where Willets had arranged for the raiders to take over.

Very possibly, Grady concluded, the driver had stopped to light his lamps. He listened, but he could hear nothing up front. He'd picked up the Colt gun when the stage had stopped, but he put it down again, and then the canvas flap above him was suddenly flung up and a lantern shone in his face. The barrel of a gun was close beside the lantern, and Willets, who held the gun, was saying softly, "Just hold it, Mulvane."

Grady looked at him, lying on his side. The gun was inches from his hand, but he knew that Willets could put three bullets into his body before his hand could move. He realized, too, that Willets had known about his being in the boot all the while, but had cleverly pretended that he was being fooled until he was ready to show his hand.

"Slide out," Willets ordered, "and don't make a sound." He reached forward, then, and picked up the gun near Grady's face, and tossed it away.

Grady slid out of the boot, stiff from his cramped position, and angry with himself that the plan had backfired. He wondered what Ben Champion would

144

do. The chances were that Ben was not close enough to know what was going on now.

"Walk," Willets murmured. He nodded his head toward the side of the road.

The driver was still up on the box, but one of the passengers was calling from the window, asking why they had stopped.

Willets was a hardcase, and he couldn't afford to let a drifter by the name of Mulvane upset his plans. There would be a single shot back off the road, and then Willets would come back with the news that he'd seen and shot at a deer or some other animal, and missed. Only he would not have missed, not at three-foot range, and with Grady's back in front of him.

Willets prodded him with the barrel of the gun, and Grady walked. They'd picked a good spot to stop. There was high brush along the road on either side, and a few feet off the road they were already concealed.

"Hurry it up," Willets hissed.

Grady figured that they would go at least fifty or a hundred feet from the stage road, and he had that much time to make his play if he were to make one at all. It wasn't much time to live, and he knew very definitely that that was about all he had — those fifty or so feet of walking.

He considered whirling suddenly on Willets and grabbing for his gun, and on a lesser man it may have worked; but Willets had cleverly dropped back another step so that Grady would have had to take at least two steps to reach him, and a man like Willets did not miss, and did not become flustered.

Grady couldn't run, either, because he was still in the patch of light cast by the lantern Willets carried in his free hand.

Grady said over his shoulder, "You're the Wells Fargo man?"

"Don't be a damned fool," Willets snapped. Then he stopped and said quickly, "Hold it."

Both of them had distinctly heard someone coming through the brush after them.

Willets said, "Don't make a move, Mulvane, or you're dead."

Grady assumed it was the driver coming up to be in on the kill, or to see to it that there was no slip-up. Apparently Willets thought the same thing, and he called sharply, "That you, Kramer?"

It wasn't Kramer; it was Lorna Greene, and she said, almost regretfully, "No, Mr. Willets."

She was standing less than twenty feet from him, but out of the patch of light cast by the lantern in Willets's hand. Grady had turned to look back, but he could see only a vague shape in the darkness.

Then orange flame leaped out of the darkness; Willets took a step back, and Grady could hear him gasp as he did so. He didn't fall immediately, and he retained his grip on the lantern in his hand as if it were a very precious thing. Then he tried to set the lantern down on the ground, but he was acting like a drunken man now, staggering a little, his weight seemingly unequally distributed.

Watching him, it seemed to Grady that the most important task this man had in life was to get the

146

lantern down on the ground without overturning it. When he finally got it down, the life had about drained out of him. The bullet from Lorna Greene's derringer had taken him in the middle.

He huddled over the lantern as if trying to shield it, and then he fell sideways, and he lay still, his arms outstretched, pale face gleaming in the light from the lantern.

Grady stepped forward quickly and took the gun from his hand just as Lorna Greene came into the light.

"He was going to kill you," she said. "I couldn't wait."

Grady nodded. "There's another one back at the stage," he said, and he started forward with the gun in one hand, and the lantern in the other. "Stay back here," he called over his shoulder.

Nearing the road, he set the lantern down and went forward, swinging around toward the front of the stage. The two male passengers who had been riding with Lorna had gotten out, hearing the shot, and they were standing in the road. One of them was telling the driver that his lady passenger had gone off into the darkness.

Kramer, the driver, was coming down off the box when Grady stepped out into the road, gun in hand.

"This way, mister," Grady called to him softly.

The stubby man had a gun in the holster at his side, and he was as quick as a cat as he leaped to one side, and then whirled and fired at Grady, the ball nicking Grady's shirt.

Grady fired twice with Willets' gun, and both bullets went home. Kramer spun and dropped into the dust.

Immediately, both passengers backed up toward the stage, holding their hands over their heads, thinking it was a holdup.

Grady walked forward, gun ready. When he rolled Kramer's body over, he could see that the man was dead. He called for Lorna Greene to come out, then, and she was coming into the road with the lantern when they heard two horsemen pounding toward them.

"Get back," he yelled to the girl, and he waved the frightened passengers into the coach again.

He hoped that one of the horses would be carrying Ben Champion, and the other would be his gray, but when the two riders swept up toward the coach he saw that they had handkerchiefs across their faces. This, then, was the real raid.

Grady stepped back off the road, knowing that he had the advantage this time. The two raiders were coming up, thinking that Willets and Kramer were on the box. But both men were dead, and they'd ridden into a pocket. Already, Grady could hear Ben Champion driving in, heading toward them from the opposite side of the road.

The two riders stopped, suspicious when they saw that the box was empty.

"Kramer?" one of them called sharply, and Grady recognized the voice as that of Ed Grubaker. Very possibly, the man with him was Buck Neil, and Grady wanted to meet these two quite badly.

"All right, Grubaker," Grady said softly.

Grubaker fired at the sound of his voice, and Grady's gun went off at almost the same time, but the other

148

rider's horse had suddenly moved and was cutting across the path of the bullet.

The rider slumped in the saddle, and Grubaker gave the spurs to his horse and headed east, bent low in the saddle. He was gone just as Ben Champion cut out into the road, gun in hand.

"Grady?" Champion yelled.

"There's one of them," Grady told him, pointing down the road. "Grubaker." The other man had fallen into the road and lay still.

"Where's Willets and the driver?" the sheriff wanted to know. "I saw Willets up on the box this afternoon."

"Shot by a lady," Grady murmured, and he turned and walked down to where Lorna Greene was standing at the far end of the stage. "You all right?" he asked her.

"I'm all right, Grady," she said. "But I killed a man."

Grady stared at her in the shadows. "I'm obliged to you again," he said. "He was going to put a bullet in my back."

"I don't regret killing him," she said.

They went back to find Ben Champion bent over the raider whom Grady had shot from the saddle.

"Neil?" Grady asked.

"Buck Neil," Champion nodded. "Plumb center. You get the driver, too?"

"He was mixed up," Grady said. "He'd thought Willets had gotten me."

He explained, then, how Willets had known all along that he was in the rear boot of the stage, and then had come for him when he was ready.

"They'd planned the raid for somewhere up ahead," he stated. "Grubaker and Neil were waiting. They came on when they heard the shots down here."

"Now Grubaker's gone on back to Bottle Springs to warn the others," Champion scowled.

"Who are the others?" Grady wanted to know.

Ben Champion took a deep breath. "One of them you know," he said slowly.

"Lace Madison," Grady said.

"Lace was in it," Champion nodded, "and doing most of the planning, I would think."

"Some of the others are here," Grady said. "Willets, Neil, the driver, Grubaker."

"One of them's not here," Champion told him bitterly.

"Who?" Grady asked.

"Jim Lamonte," Ben Champion said, and his voice was tired and dead.

CHAPTER
FOURTEEN

They'd turned the stage around and were heading back toward Bottle Springs, Grady handling the ribbons, and Ben Champion beside him on the box. They'd decided to bring the stage back to the nearest swing station and have the driver take it on back to Bottle Springs while Grady and the sheriff rode out after Grubaker.

"You figure Madison will run?" Grady asked as they rode along.

Ben shook his head. "He doesn't know how much we know, or if we know anything," the sheriff stated. "Grubaker knows that you were there, and that you shot up Neil and Willets. That'll be all he can tell Madison, because that's all he knows. That won't make Madison run."

They rode on for some time in silence, and then Grady said, "You say you suspected Jim Lamonte for some time?"

"Been wondering about him." Champion scowled. "He's an intelligent man, and he should have been able to see how things were going and take some steps to stop them. He had his chance to hire you as shotgun messenger, but he stuck with men like Neil. I was sure, then, that he was implicated." He added dully, "I didn't have any proof, though, until I wired the Wells Fargo Chicago office and found out that they'd never sent out the new man to take the place of the agent who'd been shot, and that Lamonte had not even wired them that their man had been killed, even though he'd told me he had."

"Why did he do it?" Grady wanted to know.

Champion shrugged. "Money," he said. "They all do it for the same reason. Jim was losing out with Lamonte Line. He made it up ten-fold when he started rifling the Wells Fargo treasure chests he'd contracted to deliver safely. I'll wager, though, that Lace Madison put the bug in his ear."

They were rolling into the yard of the Lamonte station at Cheyenne Ridge, and the sleepy-eyed attendant rolled out of his hut, staring in astonishment at an eastbound going through at this hour of the evening.

Ben Champion said to the man, "Ever handle a stage?"

"Used to drive once," the attendant told him.

"Take this rig back to Bottle Springs," Champion ordered. "We're going on ahead."

They untied their horses from the rear boot and got into the saddles. Grady rode up to the window of the stage where Lorna Greene was sitting, telling her what they were going to do.

"Reckon you'll be coming back into town around midnight," he said. "I'll wait for the stage and see that you're taken care of."

"You wouldn't have to." She smiled at him in the darkness.

"Maybe," Grady Mulvane said evenly, "I want to."

Lorna was staring at him. "I'm sorry for Judith Lamonte," she said. "It'll be a hard blow for her."

"She'll get over it," Grady told her. "She has Ben around."

Lorna hesitated. "I see," she said. "Please be careful, Grady. Will there be gunplay again?"

"That's up to Madison and Grubaker," Grady said. "I'll wait for you."

He rode off with Ben Champion, and Ben was very silent. Grady, knowing what was on the man's mind, left him to his own thoughts.

It was past ten o'clock when they paused at Elder Creek station to breathe the horses. Tom O'Hara had turned in for the night, but he got up to push the coffee pot on the stove, and to listen to Grady's brief account of the fight on the other side of Cheyenne Ridge station.

"That damn Willets was a smart one," O'Hara muttered. "Never let on that he knew you were in the boot. You say the girl shot him?"

"Dead center," Grady told him. "Willets never knew what hit him. She had the drop on him, and she figured she had to get him fast or he'd get the two of us."

"Killed a man to save you," Tom O'Hara murmured. "You got a woman there, Grady."

Grady didn't say anything to that. He watched Ben Champion sip his coffee on the other side of the room, the lamplight shining on his tense, almost haggard face. He didn't envy Champion tonight.

"Be tough on Lamonte's sister," O' Hara said. "I figured, though, that Jim kind of knew what was goin' on. He made it too easy for them raiders."

"You see Grubaker go by?" Champion asked him.

"Rider went by," O'Hara told him. "Didn't stop."

"How long ago?"

"Could be less than an hour," O'Hara said.

Ben Champion put his coffee cup down. "Let's ride," he said to Grady. There was a devil on Ben Champion's back tonight, and it would not let him rest.

"Pushin' them horses pretty hard," O'Hara observed.

"Saddle us up two fresh ones," Champion scowled, and O'Hara shrugged and went out.

Grady sat on the edge of his bunk, looking down at the floor and rubbing his hands.

"How bad can it be for Jim Lamonte?" he asked.

"Damned bad," Champion told him dully. "A Wells Fargo man was shot to death, besides all the holdups."

"I wouldn't figure Lamonte was behind that," Grady said. "He wasn't a killer."

"He was in with them," Champion said tersely. "The hell of it is that I always liked Jim."

"He was in the wrong business," Grady observed. "A man who knew his way around could have made money with Lamonte Line."

Champion nodded glumly. "Too late for that now," he said.

Tom O'Hara came around with the horses. They went outside, and O'Hara said to Grady, "You say that

154

woman's comin' in with the stage an' goin' back to Bottle Springs?"

"They're coming in," Grady nodded.

"I'm an old man," O'Hara said quietly. "Listen to me. Don't let her get away."

Grady didn't say anything to that. They took the stage road back toward Bottle Springs, neither man having much to say now, but when they raised the lights of the town at nearly eleven o'clock, Grady said, "We ride right in and let them know we're here?"

"Swing around," Champion told him, "and leave our horses in the alley next to the Cheyenne Saloon."

"Who do we see first?"

Ben Champion took a deep breath. "Lamonte," he said.

"You're the law," Grady murmured. He knew, though, that Ben Champion wished he weren't, tonight.

They circled Bottle Springs, coming in from the north end of town, and rode quietly into the alley next to the Cheyenne.

Champion said, "We can go around through the rear of the Lamonte yard and then come up on Lamonte's house. I don't figure he'll be in the office at this hour."

"Couldn't you wait till morning?" Grady asked, "as far as Lamonte goes? He won't run, will he?"

"It can't wait till morning," Champion growled, and Grady realized that his devil was still riding him.

They left the horses in the alley and then moved back to the far end of the alley and turned left in the direction of the Lamonte yard and office. They didn't expect to find a light in the office at this hour of the night, but a lamp was burning, and Champion pulled up.

"Figure he's still here?" Grady asked softly.

"He'd never leave a light on," Champion said. "Never saw him stay around so late before, though."

They had to climb a fence to get into the Lamonte yard, and as they were moving past one of the sheds a man suddenly called out, "Who the hell is that?"

"All right, Fred," Champion said. "Go back to sleep." He said to Grady, "Old man sleeps in the shed and keeps an eye out for prowlers."

The night watchman came out of his shed, sleepy-eyed, and he said to Champion, "That you, Sheriff?"

"Come easy," Champion told him.

"Thought I heard a shot a while back," Fred said. "Got up an' had a look around. Must of been dreamin'. Lamonte's still over in the office. I can see him at his desk."

"All right, Fred," Champion nodded. "Go back to sleep."

The watchman left them, and they walked quietly toward, the back door of the office. It was the same door at which Grady had seen Willets standing the afternoon he'd come looking for Grubaker and Neil.

They moved around to one of the windows and looked in. They could see Jim Lamonte sitting at his desk.

"All right," Champion murmured.

Walking toward the door, they pushed their way in, Grady wondering if he ought to have his gun in his

156

hand, and feeling awkward about the whole business. He knew, though, that Lamonte was not a fighting man. He'd never seen him even carrying a gun.

Lamonte didn't turn around when they opened the door. He still sat at his desk, seemingly looking down at some papers there, and Champion said, "Jim?"

Still the man didn't turn around, and Champion hurried forward, then, Grady coming behind him, leaving the door open.

When they got around in front of the desk, they could see why Lamonte had not heard them, and why he hadn't turned around when Champion called. Lamonte sat at his desk at the far side of the room where Grady had first met him.

Lamonte sat very still, unmoving, and he would never move again in this world because he had a hole through his temple, and the gun which had done it, a small, black derringer, lay on the floor where it had fallen from his limp hand. His body, instead of falling to the floor, had slipped forward and braced itself against the edge of the desk.

Grady Mulvane said softly, "It's better this way, Ben."

There was a sheet of paper on the desk in front of him, weighted down with a chunk of pink flint which Lamonte had used as a paperweight. The pen he'd been using was in the inkstand on the desk.

Ben Champion suddenly bent forward and looked at the paper, and then he picked it up and read it. When he'd finished, he handed the paper to Grady without a word.

It was addressed to Champion, and was in the nature of a will, and a confession. The note stated simply that Grubaker had returned with the news of the unsuccessful raid, but that he, Lamonte, had already seen the handwriting on the wall when he'd discovered that Ben Champion had been checking the messages he was supposed to have sent out to Wells Fargo in Chicago.

He disclaimed any knowledge of the killing of the real Wells Fargo man, and he assumed that Lace Madison, who had been in with him on the deal, had made these arrangements. He regretted very much that a man had been killed, and he intimated that he'd insisted in the beginning of his dealings with Madison that there should be no killings. Now that it had gotten out of hand, it could only get worse, and he was taking the best way out for himself. He'd entered into the deal with Madison only because he was going into bankruptcy, and this had been a way out. Lee Caspar had shot the Wells Fargo man. He was clear of that.

The stage line he was leaving to his sister with the fervent hope that she would eventually marry Champion, and they could operate the line between them.

Grady said, when he'd finished reading the letter, "Reckon that's it, Ben."

Ben Champion nodded. "I'll see Judith. Wait here, and then we'll have it out with Lace Madison. I owe him something, too, now."

"Take your time," Grady told him. "I'll have a smoke out in the back."

Champion went out the front door, heading down the street to the Lamonte house, and Grady, after another look at the unfortunate Jim Lamonte, went out into the yard again.

He rolled a cigarette out there and smoked it part way through, and then he flipped it away. He was ready to move, and without Ben Champion. Ben was going to marry Judith Lamonte and run Lamonte Line. Grady realized he should have known that from the beginning. Judith and Ben were made for each other, even if Judith had not yet fully realized it.

Over at the Diamond Stud there was liable to be trouble if Champion attempted to arrest the unsuspecting Lace Madison. Grubaker might still be in town, too, and possibly other members of the raider gang. They might shoot Champion down, and that would be the end of his life with Judith Lamonte — before it had even begun . . .

Moving across the yard, Grady climbed over the fence, and then headed down the alley where they'd left the two horses. He could hear the animals stamping and moving about restlessly as he approached them, and he spoke quietly to them as he went by.

Reaching the street, he stopped and had a look around before going out. The Diamond Stud was to the left and diagonally across the road. He had to move fairly fast now, if he wanted to get this over with before Ben Champion returned to find him gone.

Possibly someone was watching from the Diamond Stud, but he had to take that chance. Leaving the alley, he walked easily across the road, on to the walk, and then up the steps and into the gambling house.

He'd expected a bullet momentarily as he crossed the street, but nothing had happened, and he realized, then, that Lace Madison was still in the dark, knowing only that Grady Mulvane had interrupted his plans to hold up the Lamonte Line stage this night. Madison would not know that Jim Lamonte was dead, and that he'd made a confession before he died; he would not know, either, that both Willets and the driver, Kramer, were dead. As far as Madison was concerned, this could have only been a one-man play on the part of Grady Mulvane, and a play which would be stopped right now in the Diamond Stud.

The gambling house was fairly crowded at this hour of the evening, getting near midnight. A girl approached as Grady came in, but he waved her away, and she had a look at his face, and left.

He didn't see Madison in the room, nor did he see Ed Grubaker, but people who knew him from his fight with Grubaker looked at him as he went up to the bar. They gave him plenty of room.

When the bartender finally came toward him, he was standing alone at the bar, and he said, "Grubaker come in here?"

"Ain't seen him," the bartender said, and he lied.

Grady could see it in his eyes, and in the sweat on his face. Grubaker had come here, and was still here, and getting ready to make his play because Grubaker knew full well that he had to kill a man tonight, or be killed

160

himself. It had gone that far, and there was no turning back.

"You're a damned liar," Grady told him, and he ordered a beer.

The bartender drew the beer and slid it in front of him.

"I'll pay for it later," Grady said.

The bartender looked at him for a moment, and then a cold grin slid across his face. "Maybe you will, mister," he said softly, "an' maybe you won't. *Quien sabe?*"

CHAPTER
FIFTEEN

Grady sipped the beer and had a look around the room, and when the bartender passed him again, he said, "Where's Madison's office?"

"Upstairs," the man told him.

Grady nodded. He didn't think there was too much of a rush here tonight. Ben Champion would have his hands full for a little while after he'd broken the news to Judith and both of them had gone back to the office. Champion wouldn't be able to leave the girl immediately and come looking for Madison and Grubaker.

Finishing the beer, Grady pushed the glass away. He was about to turn around when he glanced at the bartender suddenly, seeing his eyes lift toward the stairs and a cold grin spread on his face.

Without looking at the stairs or turning around, Grady flung his body to the right just as a gun banged. The slug gouged wood out of the bar top where he'd been standing, and as he whirled, his own gun sliding out into his hand, he saw Grubaker halfway down the stairs, leaning over the railing, trying to line him up again.

Grubaker's blue-green eyes were narrowed, and his left shoulder seemed hunched higher than ever as he stood on the stairs. He tried to get another shot off, but Grady's gun was bucking in his hand, and the first shot was effective.

Grubaker leaned over the bannister, the gun drooping in his hand. He tried to lift the gun and aim it at Grady, but he didn't have the strength. He stared down at Grady as men at the tables in between scattered for the walls, several chairs going over in their haste.

Grady waited for him to fall, knowing that no further lead was necessary. Grubaker's eyes were already glazing as he leaned farther and farther over the bannister, as if trying to see something down on the floor below.

The gun dropped from his hand and hit the wooden floor with a thud, and then his body followed. He landed on his head and the right shoulder, and the sound was sickening.

Grady looked at the sprawled body on the floor, and he was about to start for the stairs with the intention of going up and ferreting out Lace Madison when Madison came down of his own accord, a cigar in his mouth. As he swung around the bannister headpost, smiling as usual, Grady realized that this part of it he would have to get over with quickly because Ben Champion would have heard those shots and come running.

Madison said, as he came toward the bar, "I don't like gunplay in my house, Mulvane."

"Might be more," Grady smiled at him. "You're under arrest, Madison. If you have a gun, drop it."

Lace Madison did have a gun. Grady could see the bulge of it under his expensive coat.

"You the law in this town now?" Madison asked, still smiling. He took a position at the bar about eight or ten feet from where Grady was standing.

"Deputized by Ben Champion," Grady said, and he took the five-pointed star from his shirt pocket and slid it down along the bar, where it came to rest in front of Lace Madison, gleaming in the light of the overhead lamp.

"What's the charge?" Madison asked. He was looking at the star as he spoke.

"Murder of a Wells Fargo agent," Grady told him, "and maybe a dozen raids on Lamonte Line stages. Jim Lamonte just shot himself and left a note."

Lace Madison turned to look at Grady, then, and for a moment he lost his composure. The ever-present smile disappeared. He said slowly, "Lamonte's dead?"

"Over in his office," Grady said. "Drop your gun, Madison."

Lace Madison nodded thoughtfully. He looked down at the floor, and then he unbuttoned his coat as if to let his gunbelt drop, and when he had the coat unbuttoned, he went for the gun.

Grady had not expected any particular speed on the draw, because Lace Madison was the kind of man who usually kept his own hands clean, letting others do the killing for him. But his gun came out of the holster with tremendous speed, and Grady, who'd dropped his back

164

into the holster, realized that he was a dead man unless something happened. He'd underestimated this smooth, smiling man. A man who could draw a gun with that amount of speed would certainly know how to shoot it straight, and at eight or ten feet he couldn't miss.

Grady went for his own gun, hoping that Madison's first bullet would not put him out of the fight completely, and that he'd be able to get a shot off before he went down.

The unexpected did happen, however. Lace Madison made one small mistake. He was a little too close to the bar as he made his draw, and as the gun came up, his right elbow nudged the wood just as he got his shot off.

The slug, instead of going through Grady's body, clipped his sleeve. He fired, then, knowing he would never have a second chance with the man in front of him.

Lace Madison took the bullet in the chest, and then started to back up, reaching with his hand for the spot where the lead had gone through him. He looked at Grady, but did not see him, and then he lifted the gun slowly, as if to get off another shot before he died, but he didn't turn the gun on Grady who'd stepped away from the bar. Instead, he placed the gun on top of the bar, grasped the bar with both hands, and then slid down, his knees coming to rest on the brass footrest.

After a moment he toppled over on his right side, and then the batwing doors burst open, and Ben Champion came in, gun in hand. The sheriff had a look at Grubaker, and then at Madison, and he said to Grady, "Reckon you might have waited for me, mister."

"All over," Grady said.

He felt tired now, and listless, and he started toward the door. When he was outside on the porch he rolled another cigarette, and the fresh air felt good.

After a while Ben Champion came out and stood beside him, and Grady said to him, "How did Judith take it?"

"She'll get over it," Champion told him. "They were close, but she'll get over it. What about you, Grady?"

"I'll pay you off," Grady said, "and move on."

"I might have a better idea," Champion said.

Grady waited, puffing on the cigarette.

The sheriff said quietly, "Judith and I will be getting married, Grady, and her brother wanted me to run Lamonte Line, if it can be run. I think it can be run with a good line superintendent. When we get straightened out, I'm offering you the job."

Grady looked at him. "Reckon I'll take it," he said.

Ben Champion shook his hand, and then Grady went down the steps and walked slowly in the direction of the Lamonte Line depot, where the stage would be coming in. When he reached the depot he sat down on the wooden bench out in front and he finished his cigarette, and then he tossed it out into the road.

Pretty soon a big Concord stage would be rolling in to Bottle Springs, and there would be a woman on it, a woman who had been willing to kill for him. He knew deep down in his heart he would never find a better one, and he was grateful for this. Luck had turned for him, and he had the feeling that from now on that was the way it would be.

166